SECOND-IN-COMMAND

NEW YORK TIMES AND USA TODAY BESTSELLING AUTHOR

MELANIE MORELAND

MEN OF
HIDDEN JUSTICE

D1260987

Dear Reader,

Thank you for selecting Second-In-Command to read. Be sure to sign up for my newsletter for up to date information on new releases, exclusive content and sales. You can find the form here: https://bit.ly/MMorelandNewsletter

Before you sign up, add melanie@melaniemoreland.com to your contacts to make sure the email comes right to your inbox!
Always fun - never spam!

My books are available in paperback and audiobook! You can see all my books available and upcoming preorders at my website.

The Perfect Recipe For **LOVE**
xoxo,
Melanie

Second-In-Command by Melanie Moreland

Copyright © 2021 Moreland Books Inc.
Copyright #1185926
ISBN Ebook 978-1-988610-70-2
Paperback 978-1-988610-71-9/978-1-988610-72-6
All rights reserved

MORELAND
BOOKS INC.

Edited by Lisa Hollett of Silently Correcting Your Grammar
Cover design by Karen Hulseman, Feed Your Dreams Designs
Cover Photography by Wander Aguilar Photography
Cover Model Thiago L.
Cover content is for illustrative purposes only and any person depicted
on the cover is a model.

of fiction, which have been used without permission. The publication/use of these trademarks is not authorized, associated with, or sponsored by the trademark owners.

DEDICATION

For Melissa who asked

and gives so much

Thank you.

***

And for my readers who wanted more gray.

This is for you.

CHAPTER ONE

Marcus

"On my mark," I murmured, my voice so low it was barely a whisper. "We go on three."

No one responded. There was no need. My men were ready. We knew the drill—we'd done this far too many times for there to be any mistakes.

I counted it down, signaling go time. "One."

Where once it was silent, in places you thought were empty, came a burst of movement and noise. Doors were kicked in, gunshots fired, the thundering sounds of booted feet and shouting filled the air.

Show time.

Every mission was a race against the clock. Planning, strategizing down to the final detail. Plan A having a backup; Plan B having one as well. Contingencies for every eventuality.

The goal the same every time—saving innocent people.

My feet pounded on the hard floor, the heavy thumps drowned out by the shouting and screaming around me. The building was so cold I could see my breath. Gunshots rang out, more high-pitched shrieks and panicked voices filling my head. I didn't veer off course, heading directly for the head of the snake.

The cowards that ran these operations always hid themselves in the back, hoping if their place was attacked, they would have time to grab what they wanted and slip out, not caring if everyone around them died.

Except we were far too well advanced for them. Every exit was covered, every escape route known. No one would be leaving this building alive except for the victims. They were our number one priority. Always.

I burst through the door, my gun drawn. As I suspected, the leader was busy stuffing money into a bag.

He looked up, hatred on his face. "You'll never stop it," he sneered.

"No, we won't," I agreed. "But we can stop *you*."

"I have something to offer."

"I'm not interested."

"You might be in this."

"Nope."

He was dead before he hit the floor.

Damien walked in, and I indicated the room. "Find all the cash. Blow the safe. Bring all the records."

He nodded, getting right to work. He had come a long way in a few years. When he had started with Matteo's team, he had been brash, hotheaded, and outspoken. Constantly getting himself in trouble with our bosses.

Now he was one of my most trusted men.

"Everyone out all right?" I asked.

He didn't stop in his work, adding money and laptops to the bag and getting out his tools to crack the safe.

"Loading them now. They all have blankets and water. Protein bars. They'll be gone in fifteen. We just want to make sure we have them all." He frowned. "The intel said twenty-one, but we only found twenty people."

That wasn't unusual. On occasion, a victim died or was traded or sold before we got here. Still, it bothered me. "Have the men make another sweep."

"Will do."

"The others?"

He barked out a dry laugh. "Dead, Marcus. All of them. You got the last one."

I headed to the stairs. I started at the top, checking the building myself. I always did. I was disgusted, but not surprised, to see how the ringleaders lived. Comfortable. Decadent. Far warmer than the other two floors. Big beds, lots of food, all the toys and trappings. The rest of the structure was exactly what you would expect in a warehouse and got worse the lower you descended into the building. The main floor was set up as a business so as not to draw attention to the real purpose of the warehouse. The trucks that came and went were a great cover and made transporting the victims easy. The basement where they were kept was barren, cold, and totally unescapable. Unless they took you out of it in a body bag.

I stopped in the room belonging to the head guy. It wasn't big, but it was opulent. I walked around, something bothering me. What, I had no idea. I had thought I heard an odd noise, then shook my head. Everything seemed normal. I investigated the other rooms, but nothing stuck out. My men were there, checking for safes, guns, or the one unaccounted-for missing person, but the rooms came up clean.

The main floor of the warehouse had a couple of trucks, some empty storage containers—all covers for a legitimate business. The basement was empty, and I shuddered at the space these people had been forced to live in. The squalor and cold. The gray cement walls and unforgiving floor. It was a place meant to drain you of life and hope.

I headed back to the main floor. "Everything check out?" I asked, unable to shake the feeling that something was off.

Egan nodded. "The explosives are set. I called all clear. I am setting the timer for twenty minutes." He called over to Leo, one of our newer additions.

"I need more wire."

"On it," Leo replied and dug into a bag.

I glanced at the screen. "No one left?"

"Nope."

I tapped the monitor. "Wait, what is that? Isn't that a heat source?"

He peered at the screen. "Probably an animal in the wall. Not giving off enough heat to be human."

I studied the screen. "That's the top floor. The room at the far-left corner?"

"Yeah."

That was the room that had felt off. "Hold off on the timer for a moment, Egan. I want to check something out."

"Okay."

"Can I help?" Leo asked.

"Be on standby."

He nodded.

I hurried back up the steps, the building now silent. My men were outside, making sure the trucks were gone and the perimeter cleared. I had an expert demo guy in Egan. The building would be reduced to a pile of rubble in seconds and not affect the other legitimate businesses around it. It would be listed as a gas leak, no questions asked, and life would carry on in the neighborhood. Egan had come from Romania, well trained and capable. I never regretted choosing him to be part of my team.

Back in the room, I looked around, still unsure what had bothered me earlier. I rechecked the bathroom and the closet. Both were empty. Under the bed, there was still nothing. I could see no hidden outlines for a safe or anything else. Yet, something still felt off. I stood, silent, listening, but heard nothing. I opened my eyes and turned to go when I heard it. The faintest thump. So low you would miss it or put it down to the building shifting.

I opened the closet door again and stood back, staring at the interior. Was there an animal in the wall as Egan suggested? I glanced left and right, suddenly noticing the discrepancy in the walls. One was set-in with a closet rod and a few clothes hanging from it. The other was flat. I went to the hall, checking the sight lines. The closet should be equal on both sides.

I clicked on the radio. "Egan, hold off on that timer until I say so."

"Found something?"

"I might have."

"Sure, Boss," he replied. "Trucks are gone. Just us left."

"Okay. That heat source still in the same place?"

"Yeah, it is. Odd—usually an animal is on the move."

"I don't think it's an animal," I said grimly.

"You need help?"

"Get Leo up here."

"10-4."

Inside the closet, I knocked on the walls, almost expecting a knock to return. But I heard nothing. It took me a few moments to find the hidden lever. The soft click alerted me I had finally located the device. Gun drawn, I stepped back, swinging open the door, unsure what to expect.

Thick bars greeted my eyes—but it was what they held inside that caught my attention. Lying on her side, a woman was curled into a ball in the corner, her hands and feet tied, her head tucked down. She was immobile and motionless. Despite the warmer air outside, the small box she was in was frigid.

At the sound of the door opening, she didn't move.

"My name is Marcus," I said, running my hands over the bars, looking for a lock. "I'm not here to hurt you. I'm here to help."

She didn't stir. I crouched down, making myself eye level with her. "I'm going to get you out." There was still no movement, no sign she even knew I was there.

I grabbed my radio. "Damien. Find the leader. Look in his pockets for keys. Look in the office if they aren't there."

The radio crackled a few moments later. "Got them."

"Third floor. Hurry," I snapped.

"I'll have you out in a minute," I promised. "We'll get you warmed up and somewhere safe."

She still didn't move—not even a twitch. I couldn't even tell if she was breathing. The bars were backed up with a metal mesh inside, so I couldn't get my hand inside to find out. "If you can hear me, move something. Anything."

It was slight. Barely a twitch, but her feet moved, hitting the wall, and suddenly I understood the sound I had heard. She'd been trying to get someone's attention. My attention.

Damien arrived, Leo following him, their faces shocked when they saw what I was looking at. Leo held the light high, and I used the keys Damien brought, sliding one in and opening the door.

"Get me blankets, Leo. Water. Now." I looked at Damien. "Tell Egan to double-check. Make sure there are no more of these godforsaken cages hidden in the walls up here."

They hurried away, and I leaned into the cage, ignoring the smell.

"I'm going to lift you out of here. I promise you that you are safe. I will not harm you."

She was tiny and frozen in my arms. Her skin was damp with sweat and cold, her bones showing through at her wrists and knees as I carried her to the bed. I grabbed my knife, cutting through the rope that bound her hands and feet, then grabbed the blanket off the bed, wrapping it around her. Unable to do much else, I picked her up in my arms and sat back on the bed. Her shallow breathing became faster, her anxiety building. I rocked her, murmuring assurances. That she was safe. That she would be looked after. I rambled comforting words until Leo appeared. He handed me two more blankets, a bottle of water, and then lifted his other arm.

"There was coffee in the office. I added sugar. I thought maybe the warmth…?"

"Good idea," I said, reaching for the cup. "Tell Egan I'll be down shortly. No timer until I do."

"Gotcha." He turned and hurried away.

I spoke quietly. "Sweetheart, I need you to tip your head back so I can get some warm coffee in you, okay? Can you do that?"

Slowly, her head tilted up, her heavy, matted hair hanging around her face. I pressed the cup to her cracked lips. "Sip this if you can. One little sip."

Her mouth worked, the liquid disappearing. She made a low sound of distress, and I brought the cup back to her mouth, letting her drink the warm liquid. A few moments later, she pulled back, and I set the cup on the table beside the bed. Carefully, I pushed the hair from her face, frowning at the bruises and marks I could see among the dust and dirt etched into her skin. Her body trembled in my grasp—partly, I was certain, from cold, and part from terror. I could help with the cold; the terror would take a long time to overcome.

"Can you open your eyes?" I asked.

Slowly, they fluttered open, blinking and unsure. The irises were a pale green, soft and mossy. Set against the pallor of her face, they were stunning. I couldn't tell her age, but the horror her eyes held made her seem old, even though I knew her not to be. Our gazes locked, and I lifted my hand, stroking her cheek with my finger. "You are safe, sweetheart. I will not hurt you. My men will not hurt you," I repeated.

Her mouth opened, lips forming a word, but no sound came out. I was certain she was asking who.

"I'm Marcus," I said again. "My team came here to rescue the people being held against their will. And I found you."

Thank God, a voice in my head said. If we didn't use heat source detection or I hadn't felt something was awry in the room, she would have died in the explosion. Simply the thought of it made my arms tighten. I pulled another blanket around her, tucking it under her chin. I opened the bottle of water and let her sip from it. The effort it cost her was great, and she was panting once she finished swallowing a few sips.

"I'm taking you to a safe place now."

Her eyes watched me, scared and wary.

"You will not be hurt. You'll be protected. You will get medical attention, clean clothes, and help. Food, water, whatever you need."

I was shocked when her shaking hand slid out of the blanket and fisted in my shirt. I stared at her—this tiny, broken woman in my arms. She had been locked away for a purpose. Kept separate from everyone else. I had no idea what she had experienced, except I knew it had to be horrific. I covered her hand with my own. "Protected," I repeated.

She opened her mouth and made a sound. With a start, I realized she had said the word "you." She was asking me if I was going to protect her.

I started to assure her she was going to be well looked after by a team of professionals. Except as I looked at her, a strange feeling began in my gut. If she'd been locked away, that meant someone might be looking for her. The danger she had already faced might not be the greatest danger she had to overcome.

There was only one person who could really protect her.

I met her terrified gaze. "Yes," I said. "I will protect you. No one will touch you as long as I'm around."

I radioed Damien. "Have the car ready. Blast the heater."

"Right."

"Tell Egan to go ahead with the timer as soon as I'm out." I stood.

She pushed against me, the movement weak but still startling me.

"I won't hurt you."

She shook her head, looking defeated. She wanted something but was unable to say it.

"Show me."

She touched the blanket I had pulled from the bed, the look of distaste clear on her face. Something about it bothered her. I set her down, making short work of pulling it off her body. I re-tucked the other one around her, then pulled off my coat, wrapping it around her body. It was warm and covered her. I added the other blanket Leo had brought, making sure she was bundled. Then I picked her back up in my arms. Her head settled against my shoulder as if it was made to go there.

"I won't let anyone near you," I promised and headed downstairs, rushing to get her out of this horrible building. Wanting her as far away as possible.

I slid into the back seat, holding her close.

"Boss?" Damien asked, waiting for instructions.

"Everything set?"

"Yep. Egan is waiting in the car behind us to start it."

"Tell him go. Take me home. Call Sofia and tell her we have a patient."

His eyebrows shot up, but he knew better than to question my orders.

"You got it."

CHAPTER TWO

Marcus

We pulled into the underground parking of the building that housed my team and me. I ran my squad from there as well. Matteo had offered me his house when he left the agency, but I did things a little differently than he did. No family was involved in my operation. I had no sister to protect, no one I cared for, and certainly not a wife to watch over. I had no need of a large house, a swimming pool, or any of the other trappings of the cover he showed the outside world. I simply chose to hide from it in plain sight.

When Matteo decided to walk away from this world, I missed his friendship. His guidance. We had worked well as a team, and as his second-in-command, I found taking on the role of leader more difficult than I had thought it would be. I felt the responsibility for my men that rested squarely on my shoulders daunting, and even after years in the role, I was still learning. Still trying to be the leader and boss the way Matteo had been—to lead my team with the same principles, dedication, and determination that he had. He was a hard act to follow.

I'd found this old building and converted it. It was perfect. To the world, it looked like a three-story, converted warehouse, filled with apartments. Cars came and went from the underground garage, lights turned on and off, even the occasional delivery appeared at the door. The business registered in my name was a software development company.

But it was all a façade.

There were apartments on the ground floor. Mine was located on the third level. The second floor was our command center, filled with computers, desks, long walls of open missions and plans, along with hidden compartments of our weapons. Every desk held a set of computer monitors that were constantly updated with security feeds from around the building. Housed in the basement was the most advanced server room possible. Unhackable, untraceable, and invaluable.

Hidden in the back of the basement was the large area where Egan planned and built the demolition packages we used to destroy buildings. He was the best I had ever worked with. He divided his time between the office in the basement and the command center since he was also an amazing hacker and, together with Damien, wrote complex codes that were unbreakable.

I had an elite crew—smaller than Matteo's had been. Once Vince and Alex left and joined him in a new life, things changed. Julian created more teams, allowing me to handpick my men. Smaller teams that worked and shared information. Unlike Matteo, who was in and out, killing the ringleaders, draining their funds, and freeing as many victims as possible, I took it one step further. I destroyed any building we went into, not leaving the chance someone else would come along and set up shop again. It also sent a message. A very clear one.

Damien pulled up to the elevator and opened the car door. The woman in my arms hadn't moved once. Hadn't opened her eyes, and the only sound she'd made was the occasional whimper or sound of pain if the road was rough. I strode to the elevator, managing to press my thumb to the reader, and bent slightly for the retina scan. I looked down, meeting the wide green gaze of the woman in my arms. In the light, her eyes were more gray than green, and they were foggy with pain.

"I have help for you," I assured her.

On the second floor, Sofia waited, her surprise evident when she saw me carrying someone.

"Who's hurt?" she asked, hurrying forward.

"I don't know her name. I found her locked in a cage."

"Oh my God," she muttered.

"She's frozen. I don't think she can talk." I met Sofia's eyes. "I have no idea what she's been through."

"Put her on the exam table."

I nodded.

We had our own clinic in the building. It was well equipped, and most of our injuries could be treated there. Sofia was a cousin to one of my men and had fixed him up once when he was shot. She became our in-house physician, living in one of the apartments and working part time at a local hospital. She was invaluable to us.

I had never brought anyone else here to this private clinic. I shouldn't have brought this woman. But she needed help, and I was determined she got it. And I refused to let her go.

I set the woman down, frowning when she tried to grip me, obviously frightened.

"You're safe," I assured her, covering her hand with mine. Even her fingers were bruised. "Sofia is a doctor. She's going to look at you. I'll be right here."

I stepped to the side, letting Sofia move in. She worked for a few moments, then turned to me.

"I need you to leave, Marcus."

"No."

She stepped closer. "I need you to leave. That's not a request."

I glared, but she didn't back down. "I'm going to examine her thoroughly and ask her some questions. I need you to find her some clean clothes

17

and food. Once she's stable, you can arrange transport."

"She's not going anywhere," I growled.

Her eyebrows shot up. "Where is she going to stay?"

My voice brooked no argument.

"Here. With me."

Sofia emerged from the room a short while later.

"How is she?"

"I got her core temperature up. Surprisingly, none of her injuries are life-threatening. We need to address the dehydration and malnutrition right away. But she's been through a lot, Marcus. The trauma to her body is extensive." She shook her head. "How her mind will cope with it all is unknown."

"Can she talk?"

She hesitated. "She can—if she wants to. She's confused, in shock, in dire need of sleep and warmth. Her throat is sore from—" she shook her head "—from screaming and being restrained. You need to be patient."

I tightened my hands on the clothes I was carrying, the rage running through me hot and bright.

"I can be patient."

"She did ask about a shower. I don't think she wants to put on clean clothes until she has one."

"Is she up for that?"

"I injected her with some pain meds, so she is more comfortable. I cleaned the cuts and put waterproof bandages on them. The abrasions have been cleansed. She would need to be watched."

I nodded, then met her eyes. "Was she…" The simple words hung in the air.

"She says no."

I blew out a long breath. "Wow. Okay, that's something."

"I'll come check on her in the morning. Anyone else need me?"

"No. It was a clean in-and-out. All the others were sent to the safe house. They're being looked after there."

She lifted one eyebrow. "In, out, and boom?"

I chuckled. "Yes."

She indicated the room behind her with a tilt of her head. "Why wasn't she sent to the safe house, Marcus?"

"We found her after they had departed."

"You could have taken her there. Instead, you brought her here. Why is that?"

I had no clue how to answer. I met her eyes and shrugged. "No idea. I just—I had to."

"Hmm," was her only reply. She left after instructing me on the medication to give the woman.

I headed into the room and found her sitting on the table, her head down, her hands clutching at the coat I had put around her.

"Hey, sweetheart," I said quietly.

She looked up, her eyes clearer of agony, but slightly unfocused due to the pain meds.

"I'm going to pick you up now, okay?"

She didn't protest, and I carefully lifted her and headed for the elevator and up to my place.

Inside, I strode through the apartment until I got to my bedroom. I walked straight to the bathroom and into the shower. I sat her on the wide seat and stepped back.

"I'm going to remove my coat and turn on the water. When it's warm, you can sit under the spray for as long as you want." I rummaged on the shelf. "Here is soap and shampoo. I don't have conditioner. Sorry. I know women like conditioner. I'll get you some."

She stared at me.

"Here's a toothbrush. Use it and leave it in here. I'll be on the other side of that wall. I won't come in here unless you call." I reached and pulled a towel off the hook. "Wrap yourself in this. I have clean clothes for you when you're done." I paused. "Do you understand me?"

She blinked slowly.

"Okay. If you're dizzy or you need help, tap the wall. I'll be right there." I hunched down and pulled my coat off her, lifting her carefully as I did so. "I'll burn whatever this is you're wearing." It was a cross between a shirt and a dress, filthy, torn, thin, and far too short. She had no underwear on beneath it.

She whispered something, and I frowned, leaning closer. "What was that?"

"Sorry," escaped her lips as she touched my coat.

I stared at her, aghast. "I don't care about the coat, sweetheart," I assured her. "I care about getting you clean, comfortable, and fed. You can sleep then, knowing you're protected."

I felt her touch my chest, her shaking finger tapping me. I captured her hand, holding it gently. "Yes. I will protect you."

I stepped back, got the water warm, then stood in front of the stream, making sure all the cold had drained from the pipe before stepping out of the way and letting the water cascade over her. I hit the button so the second showerhead turned on over her, the gentle rain flow surrounding her. She raised her hands, wiping her hair back from her face. Almost every inch of her was covered in bruises or abrasions. She lifted her face, her eyes wide when they met mine, bright with unshed tears.

I left quickly, the sight of her tears somehow more powerful than the vision of her injuries. I grabbed a fresh shirt and sweats, pulling them on, listening in case she needed me. She was in the shower for a long time, but I could hear movement, so I let her be. When I heard the water turn off, I waited. I heard more noises and shuffling, and I peeked in the door. Her back was to me, and she stood at the vanity, her hands clutching the counter, her head bowed. She was swaying on her feet.

"I'm coming in," I called and hurried over to her. "Let me help," I murmured.

She gave a barely discernible nod, and I snagged another towel and patted her shoulders and arms dry. I grabbed the shirt I'd gotten for her and slipped it over her head. She struggled but got her arms into the holes. I dabbed at her hair, unsure. Mine was fairly short, and I usually scrubbed it dry and ran a comb through it. Her hair hung to her shoulders, so I doubted that would work. Deciding it could wait, I wrapped my arm around her waist and helped her into the bedroom, sitting her on the edge of the mattress.

I crouched beside her. "Hungry?"

She shook her head.

"Sofia wants lots of liquids in you. Can you drink a little for me?"

I lifted a glass to her lips, and she sipped. It was a protein drink, high in calories. It would help her. She seemed weak and out of it, and I decided not to push her too much. I helped her under the covers and pulled the heated blanket I had added on top. Shivers racked her body, and I patted her arm, feeling awkward and odd.

"Shivering is good. Your body will warm. You can sleep. No one will hurt you."

I reached for the light, stopping at her sound of distress. I shook my head at my stupidity. She had been locked behind a wall in the dark for God knew how long. Of course she wouldn't want the light off.

"It's okay. I'll leave it on. There's water here and more of the drink if you want it." I ran my hand over her head. "I'll be close. Everything is okay now."

She sighed, her entire body shuddering with release. Tears streamed down her face, but she made no noise as she cried. I pressed tissues into her hand, something in my chest aching at the sight of her distress.

My reaction to her surprised me. I had seen so much suffering and pain. Helped terrified women and children, even men. Witnessed their fear and relief. But I had learned to cut myself off from feeling it with them. I had to, or I knew I would be ineffectual.

But something about this tiny woman affected me.

I didn't understand it, and I didn't like it.

But still, it was there.

"Sleep," I murmured, stroking her head until her body slumped in slumber.

Yet, the tears didn't stop.

She slept on and off for a full day. I was never far away, and she never slept for long. She'd awaken crying, screaming, or simply bolt upright in the bed, clutching the covers, looking around in panic. From my chair beside the bed, I would talk to her and soothe her, and she would fall back, succumbing to sleep once again, her body desperate for rest. When I could, I got her to drink some water, even a little of the protein drink, and I made sure to give her pain medication, hoping the medicine would keep her sleepy enough to rest.

Finally, she seemed to drift into a deep sleep, and I left my room. I showered fast, checked with my team, and spoke with Sofia. She informed me she'd be around the next day to check on the woman, and once I grabbed a sandwich, I returned to my room.

She was asleep on her side, for the first time since I placed her in my bed, looking as if she was relaxed. Her hair had dried, a soft honey-red color glowing in the dim light. It was unique and pretty. The unmarred skin I could see was creamy, the bruises she carried dark against the pale. She was rail-thin and tiny—at least a foot shorter than me.

I settled back into the chair, pulling out my gun and placing it in the drawer. It was never far from me, even when I slept. In my line of business, you were always ready. I watched her for a moment, my eyes feeling heavy. I had hardly slept, even before the mission. I never rested much the night before one, and since then, I had been looking after her.

I let my eyes drift shut, deciding thirty minutes would feel good. Maybe then I would try to wake her and get her to eat.

I sighed and let my head fall back.

Just thirty minutes.

A sound woke me, and I snapped awake, sitting upright quickly.

I stared at the woman sitting on my bed. Her honey-red hair tumbled to her shoulders in a chaotic mess. Her green eyes were light and intense, her gaze fixed on me intently.

And the kicker?

My own gun pointed directly at my chest.

Well, well. Things just got interesting.

CHAPTER THREE

Marcus

I lifted my hands in supplication, noting the determined look on the woman's face. Her hand trembled slightly, but she was focused.

"Put down the gun, sweetheart."

She swallowed, the motion bringing my eyes to her throat. It was dark and ringed with marks from a rope and other bruises. She had to be in pain. I was certain she felt a great deal of discomfort all over her body.

"Who-who are you?" she demanded, her voice barely a whisper.

"Marcus," I said simply.

"Where-where am I?"

I angled my head, smiling, hoping to distract her. "At the moment, you're in my bed in my apartment."

She frowned, her gaze flitting around the room, the quiver in her hand becoming more pronounced. She was already tiring.

"Are you the man they were saving me for?"

"*What?* No. We—my team and I—rescued everyone. I found you in the cage behind the wall. Remember?"

She furrowed her brow, still confused.

"Put down the gun," I repeated. "I'm not going to hurt you."

"Where am I?" she asked again. "What city?"

I frowned. "Toronto."

She was so startled by my answer, she lost focus. The gun dipped slightly, and she gaped at me.

"Canada?"

I took advantage of her shock and began to rise from the chair. She recovered fast, pointing the gun back at me, but now using two hands to hold it. "Stop. I'll use it," she threatened.

Jesus, she was strong. Determined. But she was waning, far too exhausted and weak to be expelling the energy this little standoff was costing her.

"You can't," I said.

"I assure you I can," she replied.

I bit back my smile. "Well, you can try, but it's not loaded, sweetheart. It won't do you much good."

Her focus shifted for one instant, her gaze drifting to the gun in her hands. That was all I needed. I was out of the chair and had the gun back in seconds.

I smirked at her.

"Or maybe it would have."

MELISSA

The bastard had the nerve to smirk at me as he flipped open the chamber of the gun, showing me it was, indeed, loaded. Then he slid it back into the drawer and touched something. I heard the sound of a lock engaging, and I knew I had blown my best chance at escape.

I'd known it was loaded from the weight of it in my hand. My head was so messed up, his simple statement caused me to question my own judgment.

And now I would suffer for it.

I waited, wondering what new level of hell I was about to enter. I was shocked when the man who called himself Marcus sat back down and crossed his legs.

"How are you feeling, sweetheart?" he inquired, not at all concerned about the fact that I had pulled a gun on him.

I didn't respond, unable to wrap my head around what was happening.

"Do you need more pain pills? I would rather you ate something if you could first."

"I don't understand," I managed to get out, my throat sore, my voice raspy.

"I'm not surprised. You've been through a lot of shit, I think." He leaned forward, handing me a glass. "Have some juice. It'll make your throat feel better."

I eyed it with suspicion. He took a sip, then offered it to me. "Nothing's been added."

I accepted the glass and drank it. The dark liquid was sweet and tart and tasted like heaven. Even only semi-cool, it felt good on my throat. I drained the glass, disappointed when it was empty.

"Cran-grape," he informed me. "My favorite. I'll get you more."

I fingered the soft sheets, looking around the room.

"How did I get here?"

"You don't remember?"

I frowned as I struggled to recall much of the past while. Flashes, images, the feeling of pain drifted through my brain. The sensation of being held, a low, rich voice telling me I was safe. Feeling something around me I disliked. Struggling. Then the awareness of warmth, security, and relief. Of being saved. Memories of intense, dark eyes that watched and strong arms that cradled joined other fractured memories in my head.

"You were there."

He grimaced. "I was."

Tremors began in my feet, moving up through my body. "You took me out of that—" the juice I had just drunk threatened to come back up, and I swallowed repeatedly "—that cage."

"Yes."

My voice became thick, and the image of him in front of me became blurry and distorted. "You held me."

Suddenly, I was in his arms again. He sat on the edge of the bed, gently tugging me to his chest. "You're okay, sweetheart. You're safe now, and we're going to figure everything out."

For a moment, I let him hold me. I inhaled his appealing scent. Cedar, fresh air, and citrus. It was warm and rich. Clean. Nothing like—

I jerked up my head. "You wrapped me in a blanket."

He nodded. "You didn't like it."

My breathing became uneven as memories began to burst through my hazy brain. "It smelled like *him*—the one who took me, who locked me in that cage. Overpowering, like cloves and heavy oil… I couldn't breathe. I-I…"

He held me closer. "It's okay, sweetheart," he repeated. "He's dead. He won't hurt you again. No one will hurt you again."

I couldn't stop. "You put me in your coat. You brought me here. There was a woman——"

He interrupted me, holding my face, his so close I could feel his breath drift over my skin. "Sofia is a doctor. She examined you. I put you in the shower and then to bed."

I remembered the shower. The beautiful feeling of the dirt and smell washing off my skin. Even as painful as the water had felt on my sensitive skin and bruises, I had welcomed it. Sobbed under the spray in relief and agony. Offered thanks to whatever intervention had brought the man who placed me in that shower into my path.

I met his eyes. Deep, rich, the color of espresso, with glimmers of gold around his pupils, they were captivating. They had a fire inside them, unlike the cold, empty, dark glares I had been staring at the past while.

Panic began to overtake me, and I struggled not to break. Not to show my weakness. I couldn't allow the horrors and pain I had gone through to end me. If I succumbed, I would never recover.

"H-help me," I pleaded.

His embrace tightened, and he gently pressed my head to his chest. His heartbeat was steady, strong, and, somehow, soothing. I shouldn't trust this man; I didn't know him. Right now, I didn't know anything—I couldn't be sure of anything.

Yet somehow, I did trust him.

"I have you, sweetheart. Whatever you need."

Against my will, my body shook like a leaf. Terror bled into my chest as the reality of what I had been through soaked into my mind. I began to sob—loud, body-racking, horrified gasps of pain I couldn't control.

"Let it out," he murmured. "Let it out, and then you can go forward. I have you." He pressed his lips to my head. "I have you," he repeated.

Somehow, those words meant more than anything else.

My eyes flew open, and I was momentarily confused. I was under the blankets, tucked in like a child, warm and safe. I had no recollection of getting there. Startled, I realized someone was gently shaking my shoulder to wake me up. I met the friendly gaze of the woman who had examined me when Marcus brought me here— wherever "here" was.

"Um, hi," I rasped.

"Hello. Do you remember me?"

"Sofia?"

She smiled. "Yes. I wanted to check you over, see how you were doing." She indicated a bag on the chair beside the bed where Marcus had slept. "Also, I brought you a few things. Some clothes and toiletries. I'm pretty sure Marcus doesn't have much girl stuff around."

I sat up carefully, still aching and sore. "Is that because Marcus doesn't have many girls here or…"

I had no idea why I asked that question, but now that it was out there, I wanted to know the answer.

Sofia shook her head. "I've never known Marcus to have anyone here, much less a girl."

"Ah."

"Let me look you over, and you can get into something other than his shirt if you like."

I didn't mind wearing his shirt. It was soft and comfortable, and it smelled like him. But I nodded and agreed.

Ten minutes later, Sofia was finished. "Your bruises look better, but you need to heal more. You're still dehydrated. Have you eaten?"

"No, I think I've slept. How long have I been here?"

"About thirty-six hours. You need to eat. And I want you to drink lots. As much as you can manage."

"Okay."

She handed me the bag. "Go shower, and I'll meet you in the kitchen."

At my blank look, she smiled. "It's just down the hall. The place is pretty open."

"All right."

Once again, the shower felt amazing. My head was clearer, and I was able to clean myself thoroughly, scrubbing my skin and washing my hair twice. I had been too exhausted to do much except the barest of efforts the first time Marcus set me in the shower. Sofia had brought me shampoo and conditioner as well as a comb—it took a while to get out all the tangles and snarls. I looked in the mirror, shocked at what I saw. I barely looked like myself. I was thin and drawn, my body a mass of bruises and marks. I had to grip the edge of the counter when a whimper left my mouth as memories flooded my head. The tight ropes around my wrists and ankles. The feel of the rigid collar they had wrapped around my neck that choked me if I moved too much. The terrible darkness that surrounded me. The cold that seeped into my bones, making me shiver so hard I ached from it. The knowledge that I would probably die in that cage, alone, cold, and terrified.

Useless. I hated feeling useless.

I shook my head, meeting my green gaze in the mirror. I was safe now. Marcus had repeated that over and over.

He had been nothing but kind. Sofia, as well.

Given what had transpired, I was shocked I could believe him, but I did.

I gathered the strength I had left and dried off, dressing in the clothes Sofia had brought me. Simple yoga pants and a light, warm sweater covered most of me. Thick socks felt good on my feet. I left my hair to dry and, with a deep breath, opened the door. I shuffled down a short hall and peered around the corner.

A huge room was ahead of me. Towering ceilings, skylights, and windows filled it with light. Old, thick planks covered the floors, exposed brick made the place rustic and warm. To the right was a living area with sofas and chairs arranged in an orderly fashion. An open kitchen separated by a long counter was on the far wall. There was a table and chairs, and around it were Sofia, Marcus, and a man I thought I recognized. They were all talking, their voices low and serious.

I took a moment to study Marcus. He sat at the head of the table. He was the largest of the group, his impressive size dwarfing the others. His dark hair gleamed under the lights, and the shirt he wore stretched over his broad shoulders. His jawline was clean, his profile chiseled and masculine. He held a cup of coffee in one hand and gestured with his other as he spoke. He stopped mid-sentence when he noticed me, his deep brown stare meeting mine. For a moment, he said nothing, simply looking at me, then he set down his coffee and stood, saying something to the others. Sofia glanced over her shoulder and offered me a smile, then she and the other man stood and left. Marcus approached me, stopping a few feet away.

"You're awake and walking. Both good signs." A grin broke out on his face. "And no gun. Another improvement."

"Your damn drawer was locked."

He chuckled. "Come on, sweetheart. Sofia says you need to eat, and I have food for you."

"Why do you keep calling me sweetheart?"

"I don't know your name. Sweetheart seems nicer than *hey, you.*"

"Melissa. My name is Melissa Evans."

"Well, Melissa Evans, I need you to come and eat. Doctor's orders."

I followed him, sitting at the table as he went to the kitchen. When he lifted the lid on a pot, the scent of tomatoes, garlic, and spices filled the air. My stomach growled so loud, even he heard it. He filled a bowl and slid it in front of me.

"Slowly. I know you're hungry, but you need to eat slowly or it won't stay in."

I nodded, reaching for the spoon he handed me. I dipped it in the thick broth and brought it to my mouth, groaning at the taste. It was all I could do not to toss the spoon to the side, simply pick up the bowl, bring it to my mouth, and gulp it down. But I knew he was right and I would throw it up just as quickly. I chewed slowly, swallowing the delicious food.

"What is this?"

"Pasta e fagioli soup."

"It's so good."

He set a glass of water and a jug on the table, then slid a plate of bread in front of me. He carried his own bowl to the table and sat down, lifting his spoon.

"I'm glad you like it. I'm a little surprised you didn't make me taste it first."

I paused, and he pushed the bowl toward me. "I'm teasing. It's fine. Eat."

I ate and drank steadily. He refilled my water glass, gave me a second bowl of the thick soup, smiling in approval when I finished it as well. He didn't try to make small talk, which I was grateful for. I preferred the silence right now.

"Good. Sofia will be pleased. She wasn't happy you hadn't eaten, but I told her I could barely get you to wake up to take meds and sip water."

"Did you stay in that chair the whole time?"

He shrugged, finishing his bowl and setting it aside. "Most of it. I had to check on my men and do a few things. I never left you alone long."

My throat felt thick. "That was very kind."

He pursed his lips, resting his elbows on the table. I tried not to notice how muscular his forearms looked. Strong and capable—like the rest of him.

"Kind? No. I think you went through hell, sweetheart. You seemed to rest better when I was close. I wanted you to sleep so you could recover. Simple."

I frowned. "Missy."

"What?"

"You called me sweetheart again. If Melissa is too big a name to remember, my friends used to call me Missy. Maybe that would be easier for you to recall."

He blinked then threw back his head in laughter. "Okay, Missy, it is. Have you had enough?"

"Yes."

He blew out a breath and became serious. "Are you up to talking?"

"Are you planning on interrogating me?"

"No. But I have questions. So does my boss. I need to know your story and how you ended up in that cage."

Just the mention of it made me shiver. Instantly, I could feel the darkness closing in around me. Feel the bindings on my hands and feet. The cold. The eerie silence that was full of sounds.

Marcus covered my hands, bringing me back to the present. I met his fierce gaze.

"Nothing is going to hurt you. I promise. If you can't talk today, we'll wait. But I have to know, sweetheart. I have to know how to protect you. I need to be prepared."

He had to protect me? What did that mean?

"You'll be there?" I asked.

"Every moment."

"Okay."

He nodded, taking his phone from his pocket and talking as he walked away.

He'd called me sweetheart again.

Strangely, I didn't mind.

CHAPTER FOUR

Missy

I fidgeted, feeling decidedly nervous. When I had asked, Marcus had confirmed the man I had seen leave earlier had driven the car the night he rescued me.

"Damien," he said. "One of my men."

Then he informed me his boss was on the way, and since then, I hadn't been able to sit still. I knew they had questions. I had the answers, but the thought of saying the words, reliving everything, made me anxious.

I sipped the cold juice Marcus had given me, looking around the room. It was a vast place—simple and sparse. It didn't tell me much about the man who lived here. The furniture was large and functional. A lot of wood and metal, dark fabrics on the furniture, straight lines, and bare floors. Nothing soft or homey. Very few pictures on the walls, and the ones I could see were abstracts, mostly along the same dark colors it seemed Marcus preferred. A small bathroom was off one wall, and aside from that, one other closed door in addition to the bedroom. The rest was open.

Marcus was at a desk on the far side of the room, busy at his computer. He would glance over every so often to check on me. I wasn't sure if he was worried about me per se or if he was checking to see if I was looking for another weapon. I had decided, if he had wanted to hurt me, he'd had lots of chances already, so I wasn't looking for anything but answers. I still couldn't wrap my head around the fact that I was in Canada. That was a long way from home.

A knock at the door made me jump, and I splashed juice on my hand. I stood, hurrying to the kitchen to wash it off after checking I hadn't gotten anything on the sofa. Marcus appeared beside me.

"That will be Julian. He will not hurt you. I will not hurt you. Please try to calm down, sweet—Missy." He corrected himself. "Nothing will hurt you now, okay?"

I nodded.

He went to the door, shaking hands with Julian. He was tall and muscular with a tight beard, wide shoulders, and a serious expression on his face. I had a feeling he wasn't given to offering many smiles. He wasn't as broad as Marcus, but then, I wondered if anyone really was. He approached me, stopping a few feet away. They looked to be about the same age.

"Melissa." He nodded, making no move to touch me.

"Hello."

We sat down, Marcus beside me. Julian leaned forward.

"Marcus found you the other night," he began.

"Yes. He rescued me."

"Can you tell us how you got there?"

"In the cage, or in general?" I asked, my voice tight, and still raspy.

"Why don't we see how this goes?" he responded. His voice wasn't unkind. "Can you tell us where you're from?"

"Idaho."

He and Marcus exchanged a glance, obviously surprised by my answer.

"How did you get here?"

"I was kidnapped."

Marcus spoke. "You must have family looking for you. We should contact them."

I shook my head. "It's not like that."

"It's not like that?" He frowned. "What is it like, then, exactly?"

"I was undercover. Things went south, and somehow, I ended up here."

"*Undercover?*" Marcus repeated.

I nodded.

"You're with the *police*?" he asked, incredulous. "In Idaho?"

"Yes. I was part of a special squad investigating the ongoing disappearances of young women in the area. A task force had been brought in to help with the investigation."

"Aren't you a little young to be on a 'special squad'?" Marcus snarled, clearly displeased.

"I'm old enough." I snapped. "The women disappearing seemed to be in the eighteen or younger age group—sheltered, innocent. Loners, not missed quickly. I volunteered to be a decoy."

"Sheltered?" he repeated.

"Virgins," I responded, wanting to make him uncomfortable. It didn't work.

"I don't recall hearing about eighteen-year-olds becoming cops and posing as pretend virgins until now."

I waited until he took a swig of coffee.

"Then we did our job since it never reached your ears, asshole. I'm twenty-four. And it's not pretend. The virgin thing is a reality for me."

I held back my grin as the coffee he tried to swallow made him choke.

He deserved it.

Julian passed a hand over his face. "We're getting off topic here."

I sighed because he was right. Marcus had riled me up and fast.

"Anyway, they seemed to be searching for the innocent-looking type. I was wearing several monitoring chips, and I was armed. The goal was to find out where the girls were being taken."

"And you volunteered to be kidnapped," Marcus snapped.

"I had a partner and backup. I was only one of three decoys. The team was watching and following. It was weeks of work. Living undercover. Establishing a fake life."

"And?"

"I knew the night I had been spotted. Targeted. I recognized a couple of the men I had seen before. I let my team know. I was ready. They were ready—" I stopped as a sudden wave of emotion hit me.

Marcus's large hand on top of mine brought me back. His voice was no longer angry when he spoke. "And?" he prompted, gently this time.

"Something went wrong. I knew my drink was spiked, so I only pretended to drink it. To let them move in. I went to the ladies' room since we'd determined that was when the women were taken. I was ready to signal my team if

I was approached, but then the world went black, and when I woke up, I was in a trunk. I could hear the sounds of the road below me. I searched for my gun, but it was gone. So was my knife. My phone with the one tracker. My hair clip with the other. My anklet removed, the silver ring I wore on my right hand. Everything was gone. I was on my own."

For a moment, I didn't say anything. I couldn't talk, remembering the terror I felt. I had been immobile for minutes as I had tried to fight the feeling. To remember my training to help myself.

"I tried to kick out the taillights, but they were reinforced. The whole trunk was. I was ready when they opened the trunk. I sprang out and attacked them. I fought, but they were stronger." I rubbed my hand along my neck. "They injected me with something, and the next time I woke up fully, I was in the basement of that warehouse. Every time I stirred, they pumped me with more stuff."

"What happened?" Julian asked. "Why were you separated from the rest?"

"When I became fully conscious, my first thought was to get out of there. If not me, one of the women. I rallied them, explaining what we had to do. I planned to jump one of the guards who brought us the slop they called food. Cause a distraction."

"It didn't work, I assume," said Marcus.

I reached for the glass, taking a sip, unable to control the tremor in my hand. Simply talking exhausted me. "I didn't even have a chance to try. They had the place wired. They watched and listened to us. I was beaten as an example. After that, the women stayed clear. Still, I tried. I figured out where the cameras were, stayed out of their sight. Looked for ways out. But there was nothing—nothing but concrete and walls. Nowhere to go, nothing to use."

"But you kept trying," Julian stated.

"Yes. Then one of the men dragged me out of the basement and upstairs. He made me sit in front of a camera. Whoever was watching informed him I was the right one—the one he'd been searching for. That they'd done a good job."

"The right one?" Marcus asked. "For what?"

"I was to be saved for him. I was going to be transported elsewhere for this man, not where the others were being shipped to." I swallowed. "I panicked. I knew if I disappeared again, I would never find my way out. I jumped up and lunged. Broke the camera, scratched one of the men, tried to run. But they caught me. Beat me again and tied me up. Threw me in the cage so I couldn't cause more trouble." I shut my eyes as I remembered the sound of the wall clicking into place and locking me in the never-ending darkness. A long tremor went through me.

"Did you hear anything, Missy? Names, dates, anything you can remember?"

"I heard snippets of conversations in the ducts if they were talking close to them. I tried to listen when I would hear voices. I heard the men referring to the big boss as Mr. X."

They exchanged another silent glance.

"I heard one of them say the name Xander, and I assumed that was Mr. X," I added.

Marcus's fist tightened on the table. "Xander?" he hissed.

"You know the name?"

Julian looked grim. "We've heard it. His name has come up a lot lately. We've been trying to locate him." He eyed me. "Nasty piece of work. Be grateful he didn't get his hands on you."

Something about his tone made me shiver. Then a thought occurred to me. "What date is it?"

"October 12."

"Oh my God, I've been gone for three weeks."

Julian frowned. "Give me the name of your unit. I'll call them. They can contact your family as well."

"No!" I gasped.

"Why the hell not, Missy?" Marcus asked. "They need to know."

I shook my head, grasping his hand. "None of the women in that basement were ones we were looking for, Marcus. And I think… I think someone on the team was working against us. With them."

"What makes you say that?" he asked, leaning close. He wasn't dismissing my idea; he wanted my answer.

"They took everything traceable—even the button on my blouse that was added last minute. Only a few people knew about that one. I mean, taking my purse and phone and ditching them, yes. But my hair clip, my anklet, the ring, and the button? Only that button? It's either the luckiest move ever on their part, or they knew what to take. They even took my shoes, and I wondered if a tracker had been in one of them as well that I didn't know of."

Marcus's dark eyes were lit with fury. A burning fire of rage. "Fucking bastard. Whoever he is, I'll kill him myself."

Julian held up his hand. "Let's stay calm, Marcus."

Marcus stood, facing Julian. "Calm down? *Calm down?* You didn't see her in that cage, Julian. You didn't pull her out of that wall. Tied up like an animal. She would have died if I hadn't followed my gut. Fucking blown up and no one would have known." He slammed his hand on the table. "I think about that over and over in my mind. And now knowing that lowlife Xander might be involved? That she was on his radar? Don't you dare fucking tell me to calm down."

Julian held up his hands. "Relax, Marcus. I'm not the enemy here. We'll take her somewhere safe and——"

Marcus cut him off, towering over him, furious. "She isn't going anywhere. No one can protect her the way I can. Nothing or no one is going to touch her while I'm around." He bent low, almost hissing in Julian's face. "And you aren't fucking taking her. Do you understand me?"

Julian studied him for a moment, then nodded.

Marcus stormed from the room, and I heard the slam of a door. I stared after him, shocked at the fury in his voice, the fear and loathing I felt rolling off him. I turned to look at Julian.

"Wow," I whispered.

"Fuck. Lightning has struck twice." He laughed dryly. "Who knew?"

"Um, sorry?"

He stood. "It's Matteo and Evie all over again. Except Marcus is far more hotheaded and intense." He snorted. "And that's saying something. I'm going downstairs. When the hulk reappears, tell him where I am. We can talk when he's calmer." He paused at the door. "I agree with you, Missy. You're safer if we don't tell anyone. But do you have family you want to get word to?"

I thought of my small apartment. My fairly empty life.

"No."

He frowned but didn't push the issue. "All right. We'll speak later."

Then he left me alone.

CHAPTER FIVE

Marcus

I felt as if I was going to come out of my skin, I was so tightly wound. Hearing the name Xander had brought it all to a head. He was a snake, one we'd spy and move in on, only for him to disappear into the grass, hidden once again. He was ruthless, cruel, and liked to sell young women on the black market. He was also rumored to keep some for himself—until he grew tired of them. I'd been chasing him for a year. If we cut off one head, another sprang up. It was endless. The only way to end it was to end him.

Simply the thought that Missy had come close to falling into his hands made me rage. I stepped in front of the heavy hanging bag in the small room I used as a place to burn off steam, and I began to hit. The solid feel of the bag under my gloved fists helped release some of the excessive energy I was struggling with, and I lost myself to the sensation, picturing the elusive Xander in front of me. It was him I beat. Him my fists punished. Time flew by as I dripped sweat, anger, and fear, finally stopping when my hands ached and my breathing was rough.

I leaned on the bag, my chest heaving.

What hand of fate stepped in and led me to Missy? Our plans had been to hit the warehouse two days later than we did. But it had felt wrong, and I'd decided to move up the date. That same feeling had struck me inside the building and led me to her. The pull I felt toward her was as strange as it was intense. In both cases, if I hadn't listened to my gut, I would have lost her—I would have never understood the feeling that existed somewhere deep inside me. The files we took showed they were going to be gone the next day. I would have missed her. If I hadn't followed up on that small heat source, she would have—

I shook my head to stop that thought. It was too horrible to even think.

When she walked into the room earlier, she blew me away. Despite what she had endured, in spite of the marks and bruises on her face and body, she was the most beautiful thing I had ever seen. Tiny next to me, she stood about five foot three and was a hundred pounds soaking wet if she was lucky—especially after what she'd been through. Her honey-red hair fell past her shoulders, her mossy-green eyes were riveting and shone with intellect and hidden pain. A beauty mark sat high on the creamy skin of her left cheekbone, emphasizing her eyes. But it was the way she carried herself that I noticed. No matter how she felt on the inside, she had her shoulders back, head high, determined to see this through, to show the world nothing but confidence. I found that amazing. In many ways, she reminded me of Matteo's wife, Evie, who always carried a quiet determination and strength with her. I was extraordinarily fond of her and missed both her and Matteo a great deal. He had married her the night he'd found her in a warehouse, running and frightened for her life, witnessing something she never should have seen. He'd told me later there was something about her, something he couldn't describe except he knew that he needed to keep her close. That he needed her in his life. He brought her into this world, protecting her against the violence, until it brought itself into his home. Then he walked away, choosing love and family over the never-ending chaos this circle contained. I rarely saw them now, but we did talk regularly. And when I took a break, I traveled to them to visit their growing family. I wondered briefly what Matteo would have to say about the situation I found myself in now. Then I shook my head. I couldn't explain it, so I doubted he could either.

I went to my room and showered, letting the water wash away the last of the anger and fear. Those emotions did me no good in any situation. I needed to come at this with a clear head. I would figure it out. How to protect Missy, how to get Xander, and what I assumed would be the hardest thing of all—how to get Missy to agree to stay out of it. She was a fighter, strong and determined. I had a feeling no matter what plan we came up with, she was going to want to be a part of it, and I couldn't risk that.

The moment I had pulled her out of the cage and held her, something in me changed. Morphed and grew into a new feeling. As if I had found something I had been missing. I didn't understand it, and I didn't like it. The instinct to protect and care for her had taken hold, gripping me deep in my core. It had only strengthened since I had brought her here. It was most inconvenient.

I shut off the shower and grabbed a towel to dry off. I simply needed to keep my cool and figure this out. I could do that. I had years of practice hiding my feelings, and one little woman wasn't going to change that.

No matter how tempting and pretty I found her.

She was on the sofa, curled into the corner, asleep, when I walked into the room. I watched her from the doorway, noticing how her fingers gripped the cushion even as she slumbered. Her body looked tense, and her mouth was turned down. I knew that although her body was resting, her mind was not. I wondered if she would benefit from talking to one of the counselors Julian had for us to speak to when we needed them. Sometimes getting the words out to an uninvolved party helped move the images away so they didn't haunt you. Despite her bravado, Missy was young and in the early stages of her career. What she had been through and seen would scar even someone with more experience than she had.

I moved closer, frowning at the sight of the rope marks on her neck and wrists that I could see. My anger simmered below my skin, making me tense. She was still too innocent to be involved in all this. I didn't want her to be.

Her offhand remark about being a virgin had stunned me. It also brought out some feelings I didn't want to admit to. Possessive, intense feelings I wasn't aware I was capable of.

I stepped closer, and her eyes flew open when the floorboard beneath my feet creaked. I held up my hands. "Whoa, sweetheart, it's just me."

She relaxed, her body sinking back into the cushions. "I guess I fell asleep."

I sat across from her. "Not surprising, given what you've endured. You'll need a lot of sleep, food, and hydration to recover fully."

She eyed me warily. "You've calmed down now, big boy?"

"I'm fine. Where's Julian?"

"He said he was going downstairs."

"Okay, I'll go see him. Why don't you lie down and rest? You're safe here. No one can get in."

I stood and headed for the door, stopping when I heard the soft sounds of socked feet behind me. I turned. "Bedroom is that way." I pointed down the hall.

"I'm coming with you."

"The hell you are. You're going to rest. You don't need to be involved."

"News flash, asshole. I am involved. It was me they wanted—me they kidnapped. I'm as involved as I can be."

I shut the door before she could scoot under my arm. "I said no."

She slammed her hands on her hips, attempting to look fierce. "You are not the boss of me. I say what I do and don't do, big guy. Not you."

Those mossy-green eyes of hers glared up at me, alight with a fierce fire. She was strong and independent. Capable. Determined.

I was more determined.

Something about her glare and show of spunk did something to me. Twisted my gut and made me equally proud and angry. Turned me right the fuck on, lighting up all my buttons. I had no thought, no plan, but suddenly, I had her pressed against the door, my body trapping hers against the wooden surface, our chests melded. For a moment, I was transfixed, then realized I must be scaring her. I was bigger than she was, and I was no doubt triggering her fear. I went to step back and apologize, but then I met her gaze. It wasn't fear in her eyes as she stared back at me. It was something else entirely. Something hot, bright. Longing. I loosened my grip, but she remained where she was, pressed into me. Once again, my body took over, and I spoke.

"I don't think so, sweetheart. Because here? I *am* your boss, and you will do as I say." My gaze dropped to her full, sassy mouth, wanting to kiss her, waiting to hear her snarky reply. Wondering with everything in me which would come first.

MISSY

I glared up at Marcus, his dark eyes glittering brightly under the lights, the gold flecks evident. His large body pressed against mine. We touched everywhere from chest to hips, even his leg bent into mine. He was hard —everywhere. Muscles, strength, and power exuded from him.

And yet, I wasn't afraid.

Given what I had been through, I should have been. I should have been panicking, screaming down the place for him to let me go. Except my rapid heartbeat had nothing to do with terror and everything to do with the desire that flowed through every atom of my being. I felt his fear of exposing me to more horror. His need to shield me. But even stronger was his need for me. His desire was evident and pressed between us. Mine was evident in the way my body craved his closeness. The heightened awareness I had of him every time he was near. I wanted more of him. Touching me. Melding himself into my skin, chasing away the memories of the other touches, the pain they had caused.

I knew his touch would only bring me pleasure.

Our eyes locked, desire passing between them, our bodies moving as if on autopilot. He slid his hands down my arms, his touch light and careful. I draped my arms over his shoulders, sliding my fingers into the dark hair at his nape. He lifted me easily, my legs wrapping around his waist of their own accord.

"Sweetheart," he whispered, his breath warm on my skin as he buried his face in my neck. Shivers raced through me as his lips ghosted over my skin, soothing the marks with his tongue as if erasing them for me. His grip tightened as he lifted his head, our eyes locking once more.

"I shouldn't do this," he murmured.

"Yes," I replied, bringing his face closer to mine. Our lips hovered, barely enough room between them for the air we shared. "Yes, you should. *Please*," I whispered.

His lips covered mine, soft and tender. They stroked and touched, small, gentle kisses that teased and promised. I whimpered his name, and he growled deep in his throat, slanting his head and sliding one hand into my hair to hold me close. His mouth descended again, and I waited for my world to implode.

The rap on the door startled us both. Sofia's voice broke through our haze.

"Marcus, you in there? Julian wants to see you, and I want to check on Melissa."

Slowly, he released me, easing me down his big body so I felt his desire that still raged. Our eyes never looked away as he replied.

"Coming."

"Not in the good way," I muttered.

A bark of laughter escaped his mouth, and he stepped back. "Let Sofia check you over, Missy." He paused with a deep breath. "Please."

"Well, since you asked so nicely," I retorted, walking away from him. "Fine."

He caught my hand and lifted it to his lips. He never broke eye contact as he kissed my palm. "Thank you."

I headed to the sofa, my heart racing, my lips aching, wanting the feel of his mouth on them.

What the hell was happening to me?

A short while later, Sofia sat beside me with a frown. "Your blood pressure is still very low. I don't like it. Are you drinking enough?"

"I think so?"

"I'm not shocked at the blood pressure, given what you experienced, but I want to watch it."

"What should I do?"

She shook her head. "Lots of rest, fluids, nothing strenuous. Give your body a few days to recuperate. It's still in fight-or-die mode, Missy. It needs to catch up with your brain. You're safe." She smiled ruefully. "Your head knows it, but the rest of you needs to get on the same page."

"Don't tell Marcus."

She frowned. "I can't lie to him."

"But isn't there some sort of doctor-patient confidentiality here?"

"This isn't the normal kind of doctor-patient relationship. I work for the team. Marcus knows everything. He has to in order to make the proper decisions."

"I'm not part of the team. Please don't tell him. I'll be good. I'll rest. If you tell him, he'll just worry."

"Already worried, sweetheart," Marcus announced, walking in. For such a large man, he moved with far too much stealth. "Whatever it is, I want to know." He fixed his gaze on Sofia. "Tell me."

She explained the same thing she'd said to me. I felt his gaze, but I refused to meet his eyes.

"Got it," was all he said when she finished. "Rest. Liquids. Food. I can handle that."

"I have a double shift tomorrow. If you get worried, bring her to me in the ER. Otherwise, I'll check her when I'm back." She smiled at me kindly. "You have lots of pain meds, and Marcus will look after you."

"Yep," he said. "I will."

I knew what that meant. I was a prisoner of a whole different kind with Marcus. I wouldn't be allowed to do anything.

Somehow, I knew I had a lot of downtime on my hands. I had never done well with downtime. My grandmother used to give me lots to stay busy.

"Idle hands are the devil's work," she would say.

I doubted Marcus was going to give me weeding to do, peas to shell, laundry to fold, or errands to run. His apartment was already meticulous, and from what I had tasted, he needed no help in the kitchen. I already knew without asking that going with him to the second floor where they ran their team was a complete no go.

I was stuck in here.

With him.

Oddly, it didn't sound as awful as it should have.

CHAPTER SIX

Missy

I hated proving people right, but for the rest of the day, every time I sat down, every time I was quiet for more than a minute, I fell asleep. Each time I woke up, Marcus was there—across from me on the other sofa, working away quietly, piles of files stacked in front of him, his laptop open. He would hand me a drink and a snack, urging me to drink more water when I was done. I would no sooner finish whatever he had given me then I was out.

He fed me spaghetti for dinner, the thick sauce delicious, the pasta easy to eat with my still-sore throat.

It was delicious, and I told him so as I slurped a mouthful of noodles, trying not to laugh at the look of horror on his face when I cut them to make eating them easier.

He shook his head. "Like this, sweetheart." Patiently, he twirled noodles like a freaking expert with his fork and spoon, lifting it to my mouth. "You eat it like this."

I pursed my lips, cut more pasta, and slurped again. The truth was, I knew how to twirl—maybe not as smoothly as he did, but I could fake it well—but frankly, I was too tired to bother, and seeing his reaction made something inside me want to tease him. To make him frown as he seriously tried to teach me to eat spaghetti properly. He looked ridiculously sexy when he frowned. He looked even sexier when he gave up and he fed me from his plate—perfectly rolled little bundles of spaghetti, thick with sauce. With zero effort from me. I called it a win/win situation.

He put in a movie after dinner, returning to his files. I didn't make it past the opening credits before I fell asleep again, replete with pasta and feeling exhausted by the effort of sitting up for an hour. It had been a long time since I'd felt so safe and able to relax. The last image I had was his gaze watching me as I drifted.

It felt nice to be seen again.

I woke, darkness all around me. I put out my hand, gasping when I felt the bars of the cage once again entrapping me. The moldy, bitter scent of the enclosure permeated my head. I sat up, terrified, clawing at the cage.

It had been a dream. All of it. Being rescued. Marcus. I wasn't safe. I wasn't protected. My mind had made him all up. I began to scream.

I heard rushed footsteps, and I knew what would happen next. The wall would spring open, and I would be silenced. Tied down. Hurt again. It was worse every time they got me.

My screams became louder and more frantic. His name echoed in the chamber around me. Hands gripped my shoulders, but instead of pain and torment, I felt warmth and safety. A low voice murmured my name over and again. Hushed me, begged me to open my eyes.

With a gasp, I did. I was in Marcus's room. In his bed. A light was on, casting its glow in the room so I could see. I was locked in his arms, his heat settling into me, his voice a comforting murmur in my ear.

"I have you, sweetheart. You're safe. I'm here."

With a sob, I flung my arms around his neck, greedily inhaling the scent of his skin. It burned away the memory I had been reliving—the knowledge that I was safe, that he was real, leaving me spent and exhausted. Silent tears poured down my face.

"I was b-back there," I choked out. "You weren't real. I was all-all alone."

"No," he whispered. "It was a dream, sweetheart. You're safe. You'll always be safe with me."

"Where were you?"

"On the sofa. I tucked you in a little while ago." He pulled back, tenderly brushing a strand of hair behind my ear. "I thought you were out for the night."

"No," I pleaded, still frantic. "I need you with me, Marcus. I need you nearby." It was true. Every time he was close, I relaxed. I couldn't explain it, I didn't understand it, but it was true.

"I'm not sure how good an idea that is," he admitted. "When I get close to you, I lose all common sense."

"Please," I begged, my voice rising. "Don't leave me. It'll come back."

He ran his hand over my head. "Shh, sweetheart. I'll stay."

He lifted the blanket and slid in beside me. He pulled me into his arms, his bare chest firm and warm on my back. He stroked his hand over my hair. "I'm right here. Go to sleep."

"You won't leave?"

"No, I promise. I'll stay." He pressed his lips to my head. "Sleep now."

I let out a long, shuddering sigh. With him close, all I felt was secure. His heat soaked into my skin, relaxing me more. His whispered reassurances lulled my weary eyes to close. His voice and touch were the last things I heard and felt as I slipped into a dreamless slumber.

The next time I woke up, the curtain had been pulled back, and sun streamed into the room. I sat up abruptly, my gaze sweeping the room. The door was open, and I could hear Marcus's voice somewhere in the apartment. Recalling my terror of the night, I was grateful for his thoughtfulness in making sure the room was lit. I got up and showered, still feeling the need to scrub my skin and try to erase the sensation of the dirt embedded into my pores. I dressed back into the sweater and pants and headed down the hall.

Marcus was at the table, surrounded by computers, files, talking on the phone via Bluetooth as he typed. He glanced up, his gaze meeting mine. His eyebrows lifted in a silent question, and I offered him a small smile and a nod. I appreciated the fact that he kept working up here instead of downstairs so he was close to me.

He shut the laptop, flipped the open file folder closed, and stood. He pointed to the sofa and, a moment later, handed me some juice and a donut. He finished his conversation and hung up, eyeing me.

"You look a little better, sweetheart."

"I'm sorry about last night. I—"

He cut me off. "No apology needed." He lifted his mug to his mouth. "I understand."

"May I have some coffee?"

"You like coffee?"

"Yes. With cream or milk if you have it."

He stood and returned with another steaming mug, his mug obviously refilled. I inhaled the aroma of the hot liquid, then took a sip. Ridiculously, I felt my eyes fill with tears at the taste of the beverage. I blinked them away, unable to meet his gaze. He must have thought I was an emotional basket case. As if he knew what I was contemplating, he spoke.

"Hey."

I met his understanding gaze. He tried to lighten the atmosphere.

"You're not the first woman to weep after spending the night with me, you know. I have that effect."

"Is that right?"

He nodded. "It's a gift."

A chuckle burst from my lips, and I covered my mouth. He was quick to lean over and pull my hand away.

"No, sweetheart. Laugh. I like hearing it. I want you to laugh more."

"Okay, Casanova."

He grinned but was silent as I ate my donut.

"What's on the agenda today?" I asked.

"For you, nothing. I have some meetings, and I'll work up here as much as I can. If I leave, I'm downstairs—not far." He slid a radio my way. "Use this, and I'll be up here in seconds."

"I could help?"

His eyes were intense as he lifted his mug and drained it. "No. You will concentrate on recovering."

"But—"

"I said no." His tone brooked no argument.

I hated to admit it, but he was right. The next two days, I slept and ate, then slept again. On the sofa, in the bed, even at the table when I tried to make one of my lists. I liked lists—they helped me sort out my thoughts and organize my mind. I made a list of everything I could remember about the night I was taken. About the voices I heard, the snippets of conversation. I felt myself getting tired, and I rested my head on my arm for a moment.

I woke up when Marcus scooped me into his arms and carried me down the hall, muttering about stubborn women.

He slept beside me at night—the talisman that kept the nightmares at bay. He would pull me back to his chest, his arms around me, his scent in my head as I would drift off. During the day, he was never far, and his eyes were often the first thing I saw when I woke up, watching and evaluating me as I stirred. As long as he was close, I was calm. At least, my mind was calm.

My body was a different story.

The air between us crackled with an energy I had never experienced before. I was aware of him everywhere he went. I felt his presence even in my sleep. When he was close, when he had left the room. His scent saturated his bedroom and the bathroom. It was comforting and sensual at the same time. I loved watching him work, his intensity and concentration sexy. He commanded attention without trying. He was focused and driven. I could hear the respect his men had for him and the way he returned it.

And his patience with me was astounding. Somehow he knew whenever I needed something—most of the time before I was even aware of it myself. A drink. A snack. When I needed to sleep. The rare moments I wanted to talk. He never pressed for information but listened when I spoke.

He was concerned about my life.

"Are you sure you have no family we should contact?" he asked. "Friends? Anyone?"

"My parents split when I was young. I haven't seen either of them since." I informed him. "I don't even know if they are alive. My grandmother raised me."

"And?"

"She passed years ago."

"Friends?"

I laughed. "You know how people say growing up in a small town is awesome? Everyone knows you and everyone helps? Well, that's a bunch of bullshit. In my case anyway."

His eyebrows flew up at my language.

"I came from a broken home, lived with my gran on the wrong side of the tracks, so to speak. I was made fun of at school, looked down on by my teachers and kids alike. We were poor, and I never had a new dress or shoes. Everything came from the thrift store. There was a group of kids that liked to announce to everyone else what discarded pieces of their clothing I was now wearing. I was short and thin—easy to pick on." I shook my head at the memories. "Growing up wasn't fun."

"What happened?"

"Not surprisingly, I was shy. Not many friends. I studied a lot—spent a lot of time at the library. Got good grades. I wanted to make a difference. I got a scholarship to a university, and I left that small town." I sighed as a wave of sadness hit me. "My gran died the year I left for school. I went and got the few things she had and walked away. Never went back. I studied and worked. Decided I wanted to be in law enforcement." I swallowed down the emotion that was threatening. "I finished and got a job as an intake person at the police station three towns over from where I grew up—our station even served that town. I didn't plan it, but it happened."

"Did people recognize you?"

"No. When I left, I was barely seventeen. I graduated early. I returned when I was twenty-two. I had changed, and no one recognized my name. I had been invisible growing up, and so they never even noticed." I barked out a laugh. "They still didn't."

He shook his head. "Idiots. How could they not notice you? You are incredibly beautiful."

He said it so matter-of-factly. He really thought I was beautiful. Even covered in marks and bruises, that was what he thought. No one had ever said that to me before. I hadn't dated much in university and not at all since returning to the area where I had grown up. No one caught my eye, and it seemed I didn't catch anyone's either.

Except some low-life scumbag who wanted to hurt me.

I looked away and shrugged. "Sort of explains the whole virgin thing, I suppose, as well," I mumbled then stopped, unsure why I'd brought that up.

He stiffened. Our eyes locked and held. The air around us grew warm. It did every time we were close. Every night, I felt his desire when he was behind me in bed, the blankets separating us not hiding the fact that he was erect. He kissed my head before going to sleep, his lips lingering on my skin. A couple of times, I woke to find his leg draped over mine, his hard body pressing me into the mattress, his arms tight as his breath ghosted along my skin, his head buried into my neck.

He found reasons to touch me at times—seemingly innocuous brushes of his hands, but I felt them to my very core. His eyes heated when he observed me. He absently stroked his thumb over his lips, and I remembered their gentle possession. He wanted me. The truth was, I wanted him as well. I had from the moment he had kissed me. I had wanted to feel his lips on mine again, taking what he wanted from me. What I wanted to give him. But he seemed determined to deny us both. I wasn't sure if it was because he worried about my physical health or my age. Even now, I could see his reaction to my mumbled words.

But he shook his head. "Not a good idea, sweetheart."

I opened my mouth to protest, and he stood. "You can do way better than me."

Then he muttered something about lunch and went to the kitchen. I leaned back into the cushions of the sofa. I heard the trace of regret in his voice, and I knew he felt the same pull as I did. But he was probably smart not pushing this—whatever this was between us. I sighed as I went through the facts in my head. He was ten years older than I was, a great deal more experienced, and although I doubted I could do better, maybe he was right. I was probably reacting to the fact that he'd rescued me. Made me feel safe. It was some weird version of Stockholm syndrome. Once I was stronger, that would change and lessen.

I ignored the little voice in my head that laughed.

The next morning, I woke up to an empty apartment. Marcus had been restless all night, and I had feigned sleep most of it. I was acutely aware of his body next to me, of the strength in his muscles. His sheer size and masculinity that he carried with ease. The comfort I drew from his closeness was still there, but other factors were now at play. I felt his heat, the desire he held in check that slipped at moments. I heard his low groans if I nestled too close, felt his hard erection pressed between us. He took longer in the shower in the mornings, and I longed to go join him and put us both out of our misery. Two things stopped me—his reluctance to do anything, and my lack of experience.

He slipped from the bed in the early hours, and I heard him go across the hall to the little room he worked out in. He returned a short while later and headed for the shower, then soon after, I heard the apartment door click and the lock engage.

I tried to sleep, but it was fitful and fraught with memories breaking through, so I gave up, showered, and headed to the main area. I made a cup of coffee, thinking about the night before. The sun had been out, and I had looked outside at the busy area he lived in.

"I can't remember what outside feels like," I murmured.

He frowned then held out his hand. "Come with me."

He directed me to the hall and the back stairs. He punched in a code, and we climbed the steps slowly, my strength still lacking. He opened the door and let me go first. I gasped in delight at the small rooftop garden on one side of the building. I sat on the bench, drinking in the sun and the air. Marcus walked the neat rows, bending to pluck a weed or study a pot of herbs. It wasn't big since a lot of the top floor had skylights, but it was a nice place to sit and had a great view.

"I guess you don't buy many herbs at the store."

"Nope. Puttering here relaxes me. Like cooking."

"Have you always liked to cook?"

He knelt next to a large pot, sifting in the dirt, repositioning a stake. "My parents had a restaurant—not far from here, actually. I practically grew up in the kitchen. They both loved to cook and passed that on to me, I suppose."

"Do they still have it?"

He stood, brushing off his knees. "No," he said tersely. "They're both gone." He turned his back, focusing his attention on another pot. Knowing I had hit a sore spot, I didn't ask any other questions. I stood and wandered close to the edge, peering into the streets. Marcus joined me, not speaking.

"What is that?" I asked, pointing to a parking lot a couple of streets down. It appeared busy with lots of traffic, but I couldn't read the sign.

"The Great Canadian Superstore," he replied. *"Groceries, drugstore, clothing, and other things. Sofia probably got your clothes there."*

"Oh."

"You need more. You've been wearing them or my shirts for days."

"Not like I have anywhere to go or anyone to see," I commented lightly.

"Hmm," was his only reply.

"I like shopping in small doses. We don't have big centers like that in the small town I'm from. I'd like to see it."

He glanced at me. "Maybe," was all he said.

I sat down, thinking about him. He was never far from my thoughts. As I set down my coffee, I saw some cash and a list on the table. I pulled it toward me.

Clothes

Shoes

Maybe boots and a coat?

Whatever else you want to buy—you know better than me.

Under the list and money was a pass card.

I blinked. Had Marcus left the money for me? I looked around as if expecting someone else in the apartment, but I was alone. Sofia wasn't here—no one was. She had checked me over yesterday and had planned to come back to see me today, but she wasn't here. Who else could he have left the money for? I stood and glanced out the window at the store he had pointed out. The large sign suddenly beckoned.

Was he giving me permission to walk over to the store and buy a few things?

I knew the front elevator needed a pass card and bypassed the second floor. The back one was private, only accessible from the parking garage, and required multiple steps to gain entry. I held up the pass card I had found on the table, feeling the fluttering of excitement. I was feeling better. A little stronger each day. If I walked slowly, I could go to the store and pick out some items I needed. I would pay him back. It would be nice to have something to wear that was different and I didn't have to wash every other day to wear again.

I looked at the radio. Maybe I should call and ask him. I started to reach for the radio, then changed my mind and tossed my hair. I didn't need his permission—I was a grown woman. He was helping me—I wasn't a prisoner. I could take care of myself. It was broad daylight, and I would be in public. No one was looking for me since they thought I was dead. Marcus must have realized that and decided I could go out today if I wanted. He'd left everything here for me to find it, so I didn't need to ask. I picked up the money off the table.

I was going.

CHAPTER SEVEN

Marcus

I stared at the screen, rereading the data in front of me. The more intel I found on the elusive Xander, the more desperate I was to find him. Discover his true identity and flush him out. Eliminate him and everything he touched. I wanted him erased from the earth.

To never be able to hurt another innocent. And to ensure Missy's safety.

I was in a foul mood. I had hardly slept all night, the temptation of Missy beside me beginning to be too much to resist. She was everywhere now. In my home, my bed, my thoughts. Watching over her during the day was hard enough, being close to her all the time and not able to touch or kiss her the way I wanted. At night, it was torture lying beside her, feeling her body tight to mine. I couldn't even trust myself to join her under the covers. I longed to slide my hands under the shirt she wore and caress her skin. Kiss the marks and bruises with my mouth and taste her sweetness. Hear pleasured whimpers fall from her mouth instead of the painful inhales of air or low moans of terror she let out while asleep. But she was healing, confused, and way younger than me. Her inexperience was a factor as well. I didn't want to add to her already chaotic state of mind. I didn't want to be a stopover in her life, and I wasn't sure she was ready for the feelings she brought out in me. I had almost lost it on her the other day—if Sofia hadn't interrupted us, I wasn't sure her injuries, age, or lack of experience would have stopped me. Every day, my control slipped a little more.

Damien's low mutterings interrupted my inner tirade.

"Um, Boss?"

"Yeah?"

"Little bird is in flight."

I blinked. "What?"

"Melissa. She's outside the building."

I was out of my chair in a second. "What the fuck?" I yelled.

He pointed to his monitor. "She took the front elevator down and walked out the door. She's headed east."

"How the fuck did she get the elevator to work?"

"She had a pass card." He typed something on the keyboard. "Sofia's, actually."

I headed for the stairs, not able to wait for the elevator. "Track her. Call my cell."

As I bounded down the stairs, I saw a text from Sofia saying she'd been called into the hospital on an emergency. *"Be back later. Left list and money on table."*

Obviously, Missy had found them.

Outside, I found her quickly. She was walking slowly, not in a hurry. She wore the clothes I'd bought her and a jacket of mine that was way too big, so she was easy to spot. Sofia had given her a pair of sneakers that were a little large, so she shuffled somewhat. Her appearance would have made me laugh, except I wasn't in a laughing mood. I was furious. Why had she left? And most importantly, what the hell was she thinking?

When Damien had told me she was outside, my first thought was she was doing something stupid, like trying to find Xander on her own or trying to run away. But I realized quickly that wasn't her plan. She wasn't sneaking out, and she wasn't rushing. In fact, she stopped to peer into a couple of windows, and I realized it was part curiosity and part a chance to give herself the opportunity to catch her breath. This was costing her a lot of spent energy.

My first instinct was to rush forward, grab her, and take her back to the safety of the warehouse. To scream at her for whatever harebrained idea she had going on at the moment. But part of me was curious and wanted to know where she was headed. So, I followed behind her, making sure she didn't spot me.

At the corner, she stopped, leaning on the pole for a minute, then pushed off and headed for the parking lot of the store she had asked about last night. I frowned in confusion. What on earth was she doing?

Then it hit me. The stubborn little minx decided to do her own shopping. But why? The money and list I had left were meant for Sofia—had she really thought I had left it for her? That I was giving her carte blanche to wander the streets? I shook my head. Of course she had. I had already discovered her stubborn, independent streak. Why should it shock me she saw the list and made such a ridiculous leap?

We would be discussing that error of judgment in full. But for now, I was going to let her have her fun. No matter how angry and anxious it made me.

She seemed to perk up a little once she got in the store. Or the shopping cart she pushed helped steady her. I wasn't sure which. I took a hand basket as I followed her, adding an item or two I picked up blindly in order to look as if I was supposed to be there. She never noticed me. She never noticed the men staring at her or their admiring gazes—even in her slightly bizarre outfit.

They noticed my glare, though.

I was angrier than ever at her lack of awareness. If she had looked around, she would have seen me, but it appeared as if she was blind to anything but her target. She meandered through the grocery section, putting a couple of small items in the cart, including a bag of chips and a bottle of root beer. I had snacks in the apartment but she had never asked for them, and I wondered if she had thought about having to carry them back the few blocks to the building. Or how she planned to get in since the pass card only worked on the elevator.

As I trailed after her, I couldn't help but think of the same situation Matteo had found himself in with Evie. He had blown a gasket when he'd found out she was alone in a mall and had her followed, refusing to listen to her explanations. He'd escorted her home, angry and frustrated. I had advised him not to make her a prisoner in her own home, but now I found I understood his anger. I wanted to pick Missy up and drag her out of the store even if she screamed and protested. Lock her away where I knew she was safe.

Matteo would howl in amusement if he saw me now.

Once she got to the clothing section, she looked around in amazement, then started lifting things off the display hangers, holding them up, replacing them, then picking something else. She put a couple of pairs of the stretchy pants that Sofia had bought her in the cart but seemed unable to come to a decision on shirts. I noticed a lot of what she held up was very girlie—flowers, lace, that sort of thing. She set them all aside and instead chose a couple of simple long-sleeved shirts. She had a pen in her hand, and I watched her calculating what she was spending, which made me want to laugh again. I could buy her anything she wanted in this store and not worry about it, but of course, she would have no idea. I realized what she was putting in the cart were the lower-priced items instead of the ones that she wanted. Budgeting as she went. I watched as she leaned heavily on the handle of the cart, her energy level depleting rapidly. I had a feeling she was regretting this little outing. And frankly, I was done.

Enough was enough.

I dumped my fake basket, walked behind her, gathering up the items she had looked at wistfully as I went, and placed them in the cart.

"I like these ones."

She gasped as she swung around, meeting my eyes. "Marcus? What are you doing here?"

I stepped closer, my voice low. "The more important question is, what the hell are *you* doing here? Alone?"

"Are you—are you angry?"

"Fucking right I am," I snarled close to her ear.

"Why are you so mad? You-you left me money to go shopping."

I barked out a dry laugh. "I left money for *Sofia* to go shopping and get you some more things. She got called away. If I had any indication that you'd assume it meant for you to wander the streets on your own…" I shook my head. "Where is your sense, Missy? It's fucking dangerous for you to be on your own."

"So, you've been following me?"

"Yes."

"Why didn't you stop me?"

"I wanted to see where you were going."

She blinked and looked at the cart. "I thought… I mean, it seemed odd, but the money was on the table, there was a list, a pass card…" She trailed off. "I guess they were for Sofia."

"She left her pass card in error. She texted me." I shook my head. "Only you would put all those things together and decide I meant for you to come out shopping on your own."

She lifted her head, her shoulders tense, her lovely eyes spitting fire. "I *can* shop on my own. I'm an adult."

I lowered my face to hers. "You can shop on your own when I say you can shop on your own."

"You're not—"

I cut her off, our heads so close I could feel her short breaths on my skin. My body tightened. "You want to think about what happened last time you informed me I wasn't your boss, sweetheart? There's a dressing room right over there I'm happy to take you to and show you *exactly* who is boss."

I expected her retaliating anger, her smart comeback. Instead, the little troublemaker had the audacity to glance around me at the dressing room as if considering my offer. Her eyes darkened, and she looked mischievous. Then she focused on something behind me and slid her hands up my arms, draping them around my shoulders. She leaned up close to my ear. "People are watching, Marcus."

With a start, I realized how tightly we were pressed together. My arm was around her waist, and I had her pulled firmly against me. Our faces were close, and we were both breathing hard. I looked in her eyes, watching as the fight drained out of her.

"I'm sorry," she whispered.

I drew back but dropped a kiss to her forehead first. Then to draw suspicion away from our actions, I swatted her butt gently.

"Fine. You can have *all* the clothes. But you're making dinner tonight," I said, raising my voice but injecting a playful tone into it.

She played her part perfectly, leaning up and kissing my mouth fast. "Deal!"

I grabbed the handle of the cart, meeting the eyes of a man who was obviously a security guard pretending to be a shopper. I rolled my eyes. "Women," I muttered.

He nodded with a grin and moved away.

I looked down at Missy. "What else do you need?"

"I thought you said we had to go."

"I'm with you, so you're safe. Take advantage of it." I met her gaze. "You aren't off the hook from this stunt."

For a moment, she said nothing, then she grabbed the handle of the cart from me, no doubt to help her walk.

"Put back all that stuff and just keep what I picked out. I was going to look at some sneakers they had on sale, though. It's hard to walk in these." She lifted her foot, and I tried not to laugh at how tightly the sneakers Sofia had loaned her were laced. It still looked as if she had clown feet.

"Nope. All these. Plus that jacket." I pointed to a rack. "And a few more of these." I added more leggings, as I discovered they were called after checking the package she had in the cart. "And this." It was a sweater she had picked up a few times and put back. It was pretty, and I wanted to see her wear it. "And you need a robe or something."

"Marcus—"

I held up my hand. "No arguing. Not after this stunt. Once you figure out a jacket and a robe, we'll go get you any other girlie stuff you need, then we're heading home. I suggest you do what I say, as you will not be coming back here—not until I say so. And we're going to have a serious talk."

She pursed her lips but nodded.

I bit back my grin. We were about to have a heated disagreement. I could feel it, and frankly, I could hardly wait.

As I was paying, I texted Damien, asking him to bring the car around. The cart was overflowing with clothing, plus miscellaneous shit Missy had added. Since my day had gone to hell and I was interrupted and out of the house, I added a bunch of groceries and some other items.

Outside, Missy slid into the car, and I loaded all the bags into the trunk, slamming it shut with a little more force than needed. I climbed into the passenger seat, noticing the weary droop to her shoulders in the back seat.

Not a word was spoken until we got to the garage. I handed Missy a couple of the lighter bags, and we carried the rest to the elevator and up to the apartment. Inside, I held out my hand.

"Pass card."

She dug into the pocket of my jacket she was wearing and slapped it onto my palm along with the cash. I handed the card to Damien. "Reprogram it."

She gaped as he walked out. "I swiped it once. It's not like I could create a duplicate of it."

I stared at her until she walked away. She slipped off my coat and grabbed the two bags she'd carried inside, heading down the hall. I quickly put away the groceries, then I picked up the rest of the bags containing clothes and followed her. She sat on the bed, looking pissed. I put the bags on the floor and opened the closet door.

"Lots of room to hang your stuff. You do that, and I'll make lunch. Then we'll talk, and you can rest."

She muttered something as I walked away, and I turned back, my anger flaring again. I glowered at her. "What did you say?"

"I said, stop telling me what to do."

I strode toward the bed where she was sitting. She pushed herself backward into the middle of the bed, glaring up at me defiantly. She refused to look away, her anger matching mine. I climbed on the mattress, hovering over her, dwarfing her completely. Still, she didn't back down. I loved her fire. Loved seeing this side of her. Feisty and spitting. Ready to fight. I could see glimpses of the eager young cop wanting to take on the bad guys and win.

I wanted her to take me on. I was fucking tired of fighting against her draw.

"I think we established who is boss here," I said, my face inches from hers. "I decide what you do, when you do it. That will be the first and last joyride you get, Missy. You're fucking lucky I saw you leave. You wouldn't have made it back."

"I can handle myself," she snipped, pushing ineffectually at my chest.

I looked down at her hands and met her gaze, smirking. "I can see how well you handle yourself. You're exhausted."

"I am not. You're just awkward as fuck. Get off me, you big oaf."

Hearing her say fuck did something to me. She looked too young and sweet to be saying words like that. My dick, while always ready around her, kicked up fast.

I lowered my hips so they pressed against hers, letting her feel me. "You really want me off you, Missy?" I dropped my head to her neck, ghosting my lips along her skin. "You really want me gone?"

"You're just a bully. Ordering me around. Telling me what to do all the time," she protested, her chest moving rapidly but her hands slipping around my neck, playing with my hair.

"Protecting you," I murmured, darting out my tongue to taste her.

"You hover all the time," she murmured, rubbing my earlobe between her fingers.

"I look after you," I replied, biting down on the tender skin at the juncture of her neck.

"You fuss too much," she protested halfheartedly, licking her lips, her eyes locked on my mouth.

"You're a pain in my ass." I ran my lips over her cheek, kissing the corner of her mouth.

"I thought you left the money and pass for me."

I lifted my head, meeting her eyes and shaking my head. "If you thought it through, you know I would never do that. I can't risk you."

"It was a grocery store," she insisted.

"You were alone. You didn't tell me you were leaving. What if I couldn't find you?" I stated honestly.

Her anger dissipated, releasing from her eyes and softening her body. "You would have cared?"

"Oh, sweetheart," I groaned. "So much."

Our eyes locked again, heat simmering. I loomed over her, every sense and nerve on fire and burning. Tension flickered between us like a live wire. My blood coursed wildly through my veins, desire rushing with it, hot and heavy. I was quickly losing control. She smelled like honey and flowers—the scent of her swirling around us.

"Tell me to go," I rasped. "You're tired. You're hurt. I'm too old. You're too sweet. Tell me to leave you alone."

She shook her head. "I'm not tired. I don't hurt when you touch me. Kiss me, Marcus. Kiss me, pl—"

I swooped in, covering her mouth with mine and cutting off her plea. She parted her lips for me, and I took full advantage, gathering her up in my arms and kissing her with all the passion and frustration I had been living with. I delved inside her hot mouth, tasting her fully, exploring the ridges and smoothness of her. Stroking my tongue along hers, flicking it on the roof of her mouth, kissing her deeper and deeper until we were both groaning and lost in desire. I slipped my hands under the loose shirt she wore, finally touching the soft skin on her back, gliding my fingers along her spine, cupping her ass, sitting up and pulling her over my thighs, never breaking the possession of her mouth. She gripped my neck, clutched at my shoulders, and kissed me back with her own fury.

I broke away, pressing my forehead to hers. "We have to stop."

"No, we don't."

I cupped her face. "If I don't stop kissing you, I'll have you naked and under me in one minute. I'll be inside you in ten. I'm wound too tight, sweetheart."

"Ten?" she whispered, running her fingers along my jaw and following the trail with her lips. "I'm ready now."

"I can't take you like that your first time."

She bit my ear. "Maybe I want it like that."

"You're—"

She pulled back. "Don't you dare say I'm hurt or I don't know what I'm saying. I am in perfect control here, Marcus. I want you. I want you so much I ache with it. Stop denying me. Stop denying yourself." Her voice dropped. "Make me yours."

"I—"

She shook her head. "You won't hurt me." She canted her head to the side, her fingers restless on my skin. "You would never hurt me."

With a groan, I gave in. In seconds, our clothing was discarded, and our bodies pressed tightly together. I kissed and explored her. She was silk under my fingers. I caressed her with my hands and my mouth. Discovered her dips and hollows. Soothed the marks and bruises lingering on her skin with my touch. Returned over and again to her mouth—achingly sweet when it kissed me, as opposed to the snarky tone she liked to fling my way when speaking. Despite her bravado, I knew this was a huge step for her. I wanted her ready. As desperate for me as I was for her. I worshipped and loved her until she was pleading. Until her wandering hands pulled down and her breathless voice begged me. I grabbed a condom from the drawer, rolling it on, then I slipped my fingers between us, finding her silken wetness, stroking her clit softly at first, then harder as she began to shake, her hips lifting, her body seeking more. I slid one finger inside her, groaning at her heat, the tightness of her.

"You are going to feel so good around me, sweetheart," I murmured. "So tight." I added another finger, and she gasped, arching off the bed, her muscles clamping on my digits.

"Jesus," I whispered, working her until she came. Her eyes widened, and she gasped my name, grabbing my shoulders and crying out. I settled between her legs, sinking into her before she had come down, holding her tightly until she relaxed under me, her hips beginning to undulate again, seeking what she wanted. Me. I began to move, easing out, then sliding back in, a smile of satisfaction on my face when she moaned in pleasure. Slowly, we built our rhythm, her body moving with mine, her eyes closed in pleasure.

"Look at me," I commanded, waiting until her green eyes were locked with mine. "I want to see your eyes when you come around me."

"It's so... I've never... *Marcus.* Oh God, Marcus, I can't—"

"You can," I told her. "You're going to come again on my cock. And again later. You're going to come so often, you won't even know your name. All you'll remember is me."

I hovered over her mouth, our lips almost touching. "The only one you will ever know is me."

She wrapped her legs around me, tilting her hips and changing the angle. Her body trembled and she whimpered, orgasming hard, and coaxing mine from me. I buried my face in her neck, groaning out my release, coming for what felt like hours, not seconds.

Regretfully, I slid from her, my body protesting at being separated from her. I got rid of the condom, bringing back a warm cloth, and cleaned her, trying not to chuckle at the pinkness of her cheeks at the new intimacy. I tossed the cloth in the hamper and lifted the covers, sliding her under and joining her.

I was surprised when she pulled on my arm, tugging my head to her chest. I listened to her rapid heartbeat, my arm draped across her. Her breathing was still ragged.

"Okay, sweetheart? Are you… I mean, did I…" My voice trailed off, and I had to roll my eyes at myself. "Was it too painful?"

"It was anything but. You were wonderful, Marcus. You made me feel…perfect."

I held her tighter. "You are, Missy."

"Aside from the back-talking, headstrong, opinionated side, you mean?" she teased.

"Well, almost perfect." I chuckled.

"Am I forgiven?" she asked quietly.

"We're not talking about that right now. Right now, it's only about us. Nothing else."

The room was quiet for a moment, and I looked up, not surprised to see her eyes closed. I pressed a kiss to her collarbone and rested my head back on her chest.

Within seconds, I was asleep.

CHAPTER EIGHT

Missy

He fell asleep fast. He'd been looking tired the past couple of days, so given what had just happened plus that fact, I wasn't surprised. I liked how he felt, relaxed and heavy on my chest, his arm around me possessively, his head over my heart. I was certain it was still beating fast from our lovemaking.

Fucking?

I wasn't sure what I'd call it. What Marcus would call it. I only knew it was pretty spectacular.

I hadn't gone out of my way to stay a virgin, but I'd never met anyone I'd wanted to sleep with either. I had been in a couple of casual relationships at university, and we'd fooled around, but never like this. Nothing ever had the intensity behind it that a relationship with Marcus had. Even the night he'd pulled me out of that horrible cage, there had been something between us.

As much as I hated to admit it, I was grateful when he

showed up at the store. Even with his barely controlled anger, I was happy to see him—not that I would ever tell him. He was so sexy with his scowls and low, empty threats. Threats that made me hyperaware of just how attractive he was and how much I wanted him. I knew, without a doubt, he would never intentionally hurt me. It didn't matter if I was recovering, tired, or even if he was pissed with me. When he pushed himself close, I only wanted him closer.

With his dark hair and piercing eyes, broad shoulders, and well-defined muscles, he attracted a lot of female attention. I noticed the admiring and frank stares of many women as we walked around the store. He didn't seem to notice, his entire concentration focused on me. Sofia had told me he was thirty-four when I'd asked her, which made him ten years my senior, but that didn't bother me.

What I didn't want was for him to see me only as a victim he had to protect. I wanted him to see me for me. Melissa. A woman who saw him for what he was—a sexy man she wanted to know better.

I glanced down, noting how long his eyelashes were. They would make most women envious. He had a long, straight nose, and his bottom lip was fuller than his top one. It stuck out a little while he slept, pursing on occasion as if bestowing a kiss in his sleep to someone. I ran my fingers through his hair, smiling at the sound of contentment he made and the way his arm tightened as he pressed closer, as if trying to bury himself inside me.

I traced his shoulder, feeling a scar there. I had noticed two others when he had discarded his shirt—one on his sternum and another low on his hip. No doubt casualties of the job. What he did was dangerous, probably more so than I even realized. A shiver went through me thinking of the hazardous nature of what he did and how he put himself at risk to save others, if he was who I thought he was. The thought of it made me hold him a little tighter as a wave of emotion swelled.

He lifted his head, his gaze drowsy but still potent. "Sweetheart, what's wrong?"

I shook my head. "Nothing. I, ah, I have to pee, and you're holding me captive."

He pressed a kiss to my chest, rolling over and scrubbing his hand over his face. "Don't be long." He was out again instantly.

I eased to my side so I could study him. His profile was chiseled and masculine. His skin was a golden color, not only from his heritage but deepened by time in the sun. He told me he liked to spend a lot of time up on the roof in his garden. He was a contrast to me. In control and intense with his men. Organized and meticulous from what I had observed and heard since I'd been here. His team treated him with respect and deference. But with me, he was gentle and considerate. Tender, even when we were alone. But even then, I sensed the power of his body, the sharpness of his mind. He was always thinking. Always on alert.

Without thinking, I lifted my hand, tracing the muscles on his arm and chest. He was solid, defined. Warm. I studied his face again, seeing the weariness in the lines etched under his eyes.

Did he, I wondered, ever have a chance to simply be Marcus?

"If you don't stop staring at me, you're going to find yourself at my mercy again," he growled, not opening his eyes. "I thought you had to pee."

"I just wanted you off me, you big oaf," I replied. "You're heavy."

I gasped as he moved with sensuous agility, trapping me under him once again. He hovered over me, his dark eyes glinting. "Big oaf?" he repeated, his voice low but his gaze amused. "I think you like how big and oafish I am." He nudged my hip, his erection hard. "Especially the big part."

I held back my groan. He slipped between my legs, showing me just how big he was.

"Are you sore, sweetheart?"

"No," I lied. I wanted him again.

He kissed the end of my nose, running his along it affectionately. "Liar," he whispered. "I can read you too well."

"How?" I gasped, wrapping a leg around his hip, causing him to groan.

"Your nose wrinkles a little. It's a sure tell on you." Then he lowered his mouth to mine. "But right now, I don't care. I'm going to take my time with you, and you'll be so ready for me, it won't hurt." He bit down on my neck, soothing the nip with his tongue. "I'll make sure it's nothing but good."

"Oh God, Marcus," I whispered, tilting up my hips, grinding myself against him. "I'm ready now."

He laughed low, his voice a wicked promise. "Just wait, sweetheart. I plan on making you more ready." He slid down my torso, covering my breast with his mouth, sucking on the hard nipple. "So, so ready."

I whimpered at the sensations he was causing. I looked forward to seeing what he had planned.

Hours later, I sat at the table, a cup of coffee in front of me, an empty plate pushed to the side. Marcus had made the fluffiest omelet I had ever eaten, and I had polished it off fast. He grinned, sitting across from me, bare-chested and relaxed. He had fallen asleep again after bringing me to two shattering orgasms, first with his fingers, then again while I rode his cock, with him guiding me, his own orgasm intense and sexy to watch.

"You were hungry," he said with a smirk.

I tossed my hair. "I worked up an appetite."

"I know." The smirk remained.

"You slept." He looked better, not as stressed and tired.

He took a sip of coffee, observing me over the rim. "I did—because you slept as well. Knowing you were safe and in my arms allowed me to relax."

His sweet admission disarmed me. His next words, however, wiped the smile off my face.

"No more leaving the apartment."

"You can't keep me here."

He lifted an eyebrow in challenge. I refused to allow the fact that it made him look even sexier sway me.

"You can't."

"One finger, sweetheart."

"What?" I asked, confused. Was he talking about sex?

He held up his hand. "One finger and I control everything in this building. I override every lock, every combination, every function. Even the lights and the elevator. If you think you can sneak out again, you're sadly mistaken."

"I didn't sneak out. I thought you'd left me the stuff to go shopping!"

"In what alternate universe did you think I would let you out of the building alone? When there is some lowlife out there looking for you?"

"He thinks I'm dead. Why would he be looking for a dead woman?"

"I won't risk it. Risk you. Until he is caught, you are staying here." He stood. "Case closed."

I followed him to the kitchen, angry. "What if he is never caught, Marcus? You can't keep me locked up here the rest of my life."

He spun on his heel, wrapping his hands around my arms. He backed me into the counter, looming over me. "I will catch him. I'll make sure the world is rid of him and you are safe."

Despite his anger and his intensity, I noticed how prudently he handled me. His hands weren't tight, and he was careful not to push me into the hard granite.

I met his gaze, not backing down. "In the task force, I heard some of them talk about a secret organization of vigilantes. Men so deep undercover they were just a rumor. The rumor was they sought and eliminated scum so terrible that governments turned a blind eye to their endeavors. They called them Hidden Justice. Some scoffed and said they were just a myth. Others insisted they were real." I swallowed. "That *you* were real."

For a beat, there was silence, then a grim smile turned up his lips. "I've always liked that name. Hidden Justice."

"Am I right? Is that what you are?"

"I'm part of a specialized agency."

I waited.

He dropped his head. "Sweetheart, the more you know, the more dangerous it is. The deeper you get means it's harder to leave."

I waited until he lifted his head, my nerves taut. "Are you really planning on letting me go? After…"

He traced his finger down my cheek. "I would do what I needed to do to make you happy."

"And if it's you?"

A mix of emotions crossed his face. "I'm not sure I'm what is best for you."

"Because you're older? More experienced? You deal with bad guys?" I paused. "Or because I'm too much to take on?"

"I like how much you are to 'take on,' as you phrase it. I am older and more experienced, which I think helps in your case," he responded. "The bad-guy thing, yes." He sighed. "It's dangerous. It consumes a person."

"But you can have a life outside of it?"

He studied me. "My old boss, Matteo, was determined. Driven. Removed. Then he fell in love, and it changed him," he admitted. "He gave up this life and found something different."

"With Evie," I said.

He looked surprised. "How do you know about Evie?"

"Julian said her name the other day."

"Oh?"

"He said something about lightning striking twice, and he mentioned Matteo and Evie."

Marcus frowned. "It's not like that," he muttered, but he looked conflicted. I decided to change the subject.

"I can help you, Marcus. Finding this Xander. I'm great with a computer. Tracking down leads and following up—"

"No."

"Why not?"

"I want you far away from this."

I slammed my hands on my hips. "But I'm in it. I was the one you pulled out of that cage."

"And since I don't want you back in one, you're staying out of this." He pushed back and began to walk away.

"You are such a stubborn ass!"

He turned, his eyes narrowed. "What?"

"I would be perfectly safe behind a computer. I could be another set of eyes. Maybe something would trigger my memory, or I would recognize someone or something one of you wouldn't."

"I said no."

"You insufferable jerk! I can't sit around here waiting for you to find this lowlife. Twiddling my thumbs, doing nothing." I crossed my arms. "If you won't let me help, then I'll tell Julian I want to go home. I'll demand to be released."

He stalked over, fury rolling off him. He stood over me, breathing hard. His dark eyes were lit with a fire of annoyance. I held my breath, pretty sure I had just crossed a line with him by threatening to leave. Part of me was thrilled with his reaction.

"You are not going anywhere," he said through clenched teeth. "You will be staying here until I decide otherwise." He leaned closer. "And I wouldn't hold my breath waiting for that to happen."

He turned and strode away, heading toward the room he used for workouts.

"Looking forward to working with you, then," I called. "I think it'll be great!"

The door shook as he slammed it shut behind him.

I thought I had won.

CHAPTER NINE

Marcus

I worked out until I was a sweating mass of exhaustion. Missy's words kept echoing in my head.

All of them. Her quiet question about a life outside this one. Her insistence that she be allowed to help with the case.

Her thought process was correct. She would be perfectly safe behind a computer. Damien and his team were amazing, and everything we did was untraceable. We were cloaked in darkness as we searched and gathered intel.

But the thought of her seeing some of the things I did. Reading the words, looking at the images, made me want to explode. It was hard enough living with the pictures burned into my mind. Knowing they would be in her brain as well seemed unacceptable. I knew she had trained to be a cop, but she was still so young, and given the small town she lived in, she hadn't had a lot of experience. I still shook my head that she had been allowed on the task force. I had to admit she was perfect for the role, but given her limited experience, it surprised me.

But then again, I wasn't part of that system, and it probably worked differently from what I was used to.

She was intelligent—there was no denying that fact. She had figured out who I was, what I did, and had made the connection to who I worked for. We had teams all over the world, so I wasn't surprised about the rumors.

She was the perfect mix of everything I liked, everything I would have looked for in a woman, a partner—if I had been looking.

I hadn't expected her. I hadn't expected to feel the way I did that night when I pulled her out of the cage.

And I certainly hadn't expected her to still be with me. I should take her to Julian—let her go. He would make sure she was taken care of—resettled somewhere safe. I could even send her to Matteo and Evie, who would watch over her. Yet, I couldn't bear the thought of her leaving.

With a groan, I headed to the shower, stopping in the doorway. Missy was asleep on the bed, curled up like a kitten on the mattress. She held my pillow, her arms keeping it close as if she were holding me. I had liked sleeping with her earlier, the feeling of her body tucked under mine, her heartbeat in my ear. She brought out so many feelings in me. Tenderness and desire. The need to protect and defend. The instinct to nurture and look after her. So many foreign emotions raged when I looked at her.

She could also wind me up faster than anything in the world. In my job, I had to be calm. Cool and rational. I had trained myself for years not to react, but to solve. Never show what I was feeling. With her, that was impossible. I felt so many things at once, one of them broke through every time she was around. Often, it was annoyance if she was awake. She loved to press my buttons, to exert her will, and to push back. I had to admit, at times, she amused me. She was little, but she was fierce, as if her anger made her forget her size.

She shifted, the blanket falling away, exposing her shoulder. The bruise on her arm was fading, but it reminded me of what she had gone through. She was stronger than I gave her credit for. She refused to let what happened break her, instead fought back and tried to find a sense of normalcy in this place that was new and strange to her.

Like going shopping to buy some clothes.

I approached the bed, tugging the blanket up over her shoulder. Her eyes fluttered open, and she smiled sweetly, drowsy and sexy-looking in my bed.

That was the biggest thing. The desire I felt for her. It was a never-ending burning sensation under my skin. It simmered and bubbled away until it exploded—usually after one of our sparring matches. But it was always there. I was aware of her everywhere. Even when I was out of the room or downstairs, I knew where she was—as if my body was aligned to hers.

I hunched down, touching her cheek. "Go back to sleep, sweetheart."

"Are you still mad at me?"

"No. I took it out on the punching bag. I'm going to go have a shower."

I kissed her cheek and stood, tossing my clothes into the hamper and heading to the bathroom.

"Marcus?"

I turned. She had sat up, the blanket falling away. Her full breasts were on display, and she didn't try to cover them. My cock noticed, beginning to stir.

"Do you want me to come wash your back?" she asked, dropping her gaze to my crotch, then meeting my eyes. "Or help wash, ah, other things?"

"That might lead to something else entirely."

She pushed off the bed, standing in front of me. Naked, brave, and lovely despite the lingering marks. Artless in her sexiness, filling me with the need to be with her again. I wanted to feel her hands on me under the hot water. To run mine over her tempting body. I held out my hand, smiling when she closed the gap between us and took it. I eyed her, my hunger for her growing quickly. She met my ravenous gaze with one of her own, the green in her eyes bright with desire.

I was going to enjoy this shower.

"Tell me about your parents."

We were lying in bed, the evening descending around us. The shower had been long, loud, and we'd ended up as dirty as when we started. Missy might not have a great deal of experience, but her quick learning had me leaning against the wall, groaning her name, unable to look at her as she wrapped her lips around my cock and proceeded to give me the best blow job I had ever experienced. It was as if her naïveté added to the pleasure. Something about her innocent touches, hesitant exploration, then enthusiastic enjoyment caught me off guard and did something strange to my chest. I'd had to keep my gaze focused elsewhere, or I would have blown in less than a minute if I did more than sneak a look at her. I responded in kind, and she had cried out my name, the hold she had on my hair almost painful as she tugged and rode out her orgasms.

Yes, two of them.

I gave her a third with my cock buried inside her, pulling out, before I ejaculated all over her stomach and thighs. By that time, the water was cool, and we had to rinse off quickly. She still felt the cold fast.

I bent an arm under my head, mirroring her position. "What do you want to know?"

"When did they die?" she asked quietly.

"I was seventeen. My dad had a heart attack one day in the restaurant and died in my mother's arms. She never got over it. She couldn't bear to go to the restaurant anymore and closed it. She died six months later."

"Oh, Marcus," she whispered, moving closer. "I'm sorry."

I stared at the wall behind her, unable to see the look of pity on her face. "We lived in a fairly rough neighborhood. The restaurant was a favorite of some local thugs, who kind of protected my parents. A rival gang moved into the area, and they were a constant source of stress to my parents. The place became a sort of standoff between the two gangs. My dad hated it. He always strived to be a good neighbor. Help others in the area. He didn't understand the mentality. It ate at him and, I think, caused his health to fail. I lost them both because of some young idiots wanting to stake a claim that wasn't theirs to stake. In the end, we all lost. I had no parents, there was no restaurant, and for what? The stupid concept that it was their territory?" I huffed an angry breath. "Idiots."

"What did you do?"

I rolled, folding my arms under my head. I felt a surge of quiet pleasure when Missy edged closer, laying her head on my chest. Without thinking, I slid an arm out, spreading my hand across her bare back and caressing the skin.

"I was young and tough. You had to be in that neighborhood. Another fan of my parents' restaurant was Aldo—Matteo's first boss. He looked out for me, made sure I got to keep my parents' apartment, and he got me some training. He saw something in me. Told me about what he did—the work. I found it fascinating—the thought of working to rid the world of awful people. Men who started out like the young idiots who'd helped put my father in an early grave and then moved on and got worse. Through him, I met Matteo, and we became fast friends. When he got his first team, I was at his side. I was until the day he left, and I took over his spot. I went from being second-in-command to the boss." I allowed a smile to break through. "I think most days I wish I was still his second. I miss working with him. But he is happy, and that is what is important."

She was silent for a moment. "What was the name of the restaurant?"

"Vinny G's. My dad was Vincent, and my mom was Gia. They thought it was cute."

"It was," she agreed.

She traced a finger over my chest. "And you learned to cook from them?"

"Yes. And garden from my nonna, who lived with us until she died. The windows were full of her pots. The front stoop of the apartment block too. Everyone knew who they belonged to. She even had my dad dig out the little bit of dirt in the back, and she grew tomatoes and peppers. She shared them with everyone. Taught me how fresh always tastes best."

"And you have no siblings?"

"No, just me." I paused. "It's best that way. What I do is too dangerous. I have no weak link." Then, unable to stop myself, I glanced down at her, meeting her soft, mossy-colored eyes. "At least I didn't," I admitted in a low voice.

She smiled, looking sweet and indulgent. It was a rare moment between us. One of honesty and emotion. No anger, no raging passion or fear, nothing but us. It unsettled me, even as it warmed me.

Luckily, her stomach chose to growl, and I chuckled. "Maybe I need to show off my cooking skills and feed you?"

"Would you make me pasta?"

I bent and kissed the end of her nose. "Yes."

Perched on the counter, she watched me make a fast marinara and was fascinated with the bags of fresh pasta

I had frozen in the freezer. I shrugged. "Pop in boiling water and it's ready in two minutes. I don't always have time to make up a batch, and I don't like the dry packaged stuff. Tastes like shit."

"I've never had fresh pasta, much less made it," she said.

"I'll show you."

She smiled, looking almost shy. "I'd like that."

I stirred the marinara, tapping the spoon against the pot. "I need some basil."

"I can get it."

I hesitated, and she shook her head. "Really, Marcus? You think someone is looking for me on your roof?"

I chuckled. "Fine, 631790 is the passcode for the stairs and the door."

She repeated it and jumped down, wincing slightly as her feet hit the hard wooden floor.

"You okay?" I asked.

She paused then nodded. "Yeah, I'm good."

"Basil, woman. I need it."

"Okay, okay, bossyman."

She left, the door clicking shut quietly. I diced some garlic and shallots, adding them to the pot. I stirred the sauce, lowering the heat so it would only simmer gently. I got out some chicken and pounded the fillets thin to make cutlets, then frowned, glancing at my watch. She'd been gone fifteen minutes. Five would have been sufficient, ten if she was unsure which plant was basil.

I wiped my hands, turned off the stove, and headed up the stairs. Maybe she'd forgotten the code to the door. But it was propped open the way she had seen me do the other night. I looked toward the garden, and my stomach dropped. I didn't see her. I hurried forward, stopping when I found her. She was curled into a ball, sobbing, a bunch of basil clutched in her hand. Rushing to her side, I dropped beside her, gathering her in my arms. "Sweetheart, what is it? What happened? Are you hurt?"

She buried her face into my neck, still sobbing but shaking her head.

"Tell me," I insisted. "Did you get stung? Fall?"

There were more headshakes, but she kept crying. I held her close, letting her get it out, mystified.

Finally, the sobs eased, and she exhaled a long, shuddering breath. I pushed the hair off her face.

"Tell me what happened," I said, keeping my voice calm.

"My feet. When they threw me in the cage, I tried to kick out the wall, but it was reinforced and I hurt my heels. It pissed them off that I was still causing trouble, and they dragged me out and tied me up so I couldn't make any more noise. They left me like that for days.

When they finally dragged me out again, they took me downstairs and hosed me off, then tossed me back in with a bucket. My hands and feet were still tied, but I could move a little." She sniffled. "I was so cold and wet and scared. I didn't think I would make it out of there."

"Sweetheart..." I whispered, my eyes shutting at the pain in her voice. The horrors she lived that stayed in her mind.

"When I hit the floor just now, the pain in my heels reminded me of how they ached for days. And then I just started to cry when I came up here. The sun was out, the dirt felt so warm under my feet, and then...I was just suddenly so grateful to be here—with you."

I held her closer. "I'm grateful too."

I let her settle a little, allowing the sun to soak into her skin, to warm her and chase away the bad memories.

"I'm going to call Julian tomorrow and set you up with our in-house counselor. You need to talk these memories out."

"I can't talk to you?"

I passed my hand over her forehead, pressing my lips to her skin. "Anytime. But with someone not as emotionally involved, you might get some ways to cope, rather than hearing me want to find the scum that touched you and kill them all over again."

She smiled. "My hero."

"Always." I stood, taking her with me. "Right now, your hero is going to feed you, then we can relax for what is left of the evening."

She laid her hand on my arm. "Can I stay up here for a little while longer? Alone?"

I carefully set her on her feet. "Whatever you need."

"I just want to watch the sunset."

"Okay, sweetheart. We'll eat when you come downstairs."

I headed to the door, looking back over my shoulder. She had sat back down, drawing up her legs. She rested her chin on her knees, her face tilted toward the setting sun. She was the picture of peace, yet I knew there were moments she was anything but peaceful.

Determined, I went downstairs.

I would get her the help she needed to find that peace. I hated the fact that it couldn't be me, but I also knew I wasn't the right person for that job. I could be her rock, her safe place, but I had to let her go far enough away that she wanted to return to me.

I only hoped that was what happened. Because somehow, someway, she had become the most important thing in my life.

Missy slipped her hand in mine, the palm damp and cool. I squeezed her fingers. "It's just to talk to someone, sweetheart."

"I know. I'm nervous, though. Can you come in?"

"I think Dr. Easton prefers one-on-one. She wants to make sure you're comfortable and not holding back with me there."

"Okay. But you'll be here?"

"I'm not going anywhere."

Dr. Easton came out, shook my hand, and introduced herself to Missy. They headed into her office, and the last thing I saw was Missy's anxious gaze as the door closed. It took everything in me not to follow her in there. I wanted to hold her hand and help her through this process, but I knew from personal experience she had to do it on her own.

I wasn't surprised when Julian appeared, seating himself across from me. He would know I was in the building. Nothing happened here he wasn't aware of. The small office building housed one of the most secretive organizations in existence, yet to the outside world was simply another structure in a bustling city. A small legitimate company he ran was a front—but highly successful. Employees were coming and going, deliveries and repairs happening just like any other business, and it blended perfectly. Two front-facing, main-floor legitimate businesses added to the illusion—both handpicked by Julian to serve a purpose. A small café and a corner convenience store were busy and prosperous. Like me, Julian preferred to hide out in the open. No one saw the expensive computer hacking system, the diligent teams that worked behind the screens. The hidden office he worked from. The dedicated professionals who strove to make the city and the world a little safer, one mission at a time.

It was a never-ending, thankless, unseen job that few chose to do, and always had an expiry date. No one could do it forever. It extracted far too heavy a price from your sanity.

"How is she?" he asked.

"I think this will help. She needs to talk, and every time she shares, I want to kill someone." I ran a hand over my hair with a rueful smirk. "I had to order a new punching bag yesterday."

He nodded. "You're in deep with her, Marcus. Is that wise?"

I met his gaze. He looked concerned, but not angry or judgmental. I shrugged helplessly. "I can't control it, Julian. I didn't plan on it and it has surprised me as much as it has you, but it's there."

"A draw," he said quietly. "Like Matteo had to Evie."

I laughed at the irony of his words. "Yeah, like Matteo. But at least I didn't marry her the same night."

"But will you?"

His question stopped me. "I don't know."

"I can get her a fresh start. New name. Send her some place safe where I can keep tabs on her. Make sure she's okay."

The thought of her leaving, of her being somewhere I couldn't protect her, couldn't touch her, made me crazy. "No," I said emphatically. "No, you cannot."

He relaxed back into the cushions. "I suppose I have my answer. But Marcus, you can't keep her locked up. You know that."

"For now, I have no choice. There is nothing else I can do."

He leaned forward, bracing his elbows on his knees, his voice low. "You and I both know that is bullshit. I pulled some files on her. She was top of her classes. Well-thought-of by instructors. Always willing to work harder, work more. Very adept at research." He shook his head. "She could have gone straight into police work, not a grunt job like an intake clerk. I don't know if she held herself back or her superiors did, but her talent was underused."

"What are you saying?"

"Let her help."

I scrubbed my face. "I don't want—"

He cut me off. "Stop thinking with your heart. I am telling you this is what has to happen. She needs to feel as if she is part of the solution, instead of only the victim. Let her work with Damien, checking leads, digging through files. Another pair of hands and eyes, especially one already familiar with the case and clever, is an asset. If you'd get past this caveman bullshit, you'd admit that. She'll be in the building, safe, but productive."

He sat back, shaking his head. "The tighter the noose, Marcus, the more she'll resent it. Resent you. Matteo found that out and had to refigure his thinking. The same goes for you."

When I didn't respond, he added his final thoughts. "She isn't Evie, Marcus. Evie was innocent of this entire world when Matteo brought her into it. She stumbled before she found her feet, and Matteo was right to keep her sheltered until she was ready. But once she was, he realized what he had to do. Missy has training, some background, and she wants to be involved. And I believe she is ready. You need to get over this. You're letting your fear win." He stood. "The problem is yours, not hers. I suggest you think on that."

He left me alone, his words on repeat in my head.

121

At the end of the week, I stared in shock at Dr. Easton. Partway through Missy's scheduled appointment, she'd opened the door and asked me to join them.

"Can you repeat that?" I asked.

Sitting in her chair, legs crossed, a notebook on her lap, Dr. Easton was the epitome of relaxed. In control and professional. "You're letting your fears override your good judgment in regard to Missy."

Her wording was so close to Julian's, I wondered if the two of them had talked.

"I'm not sure you have the right to make that decision," I responded.

She smiled, tilting her head and studying me. "I assure you I do."

"You think she can handle working on this case? With everything she went through?"

Missy turned to me, her eyes narrowed. "*She* is right here."

I scrubbed my face. "Why?" I asked, directing the single word to her.

"They took away my freedom and rights when they kidnapped me and shoved me in that cage like I was an animal. I wasn't even human to them. None of the women were. I need to be part of the team that takes *him* down. The one pulling all the strings behind the scenes. I need to know why I was singled out." She slipped her hands over mine. "The only one stopping me is you, Marcus. You don't trust me or have any faith."

"No, I do," I protested. "But Missy, you'll relive what you went through every day. See pictures and read things that will be burned into your brain forever. I'm trying to spare you that."

She inched closer so our knees were touching. "I already have images burned in my brain, Marcus. Maybe by helping, I could stop that from happening to another woman. I want to do that. I want to try."

I wanted to punch something, but I knew at the moment, that was impossible. I glanced at Dr. Easton, who was watching us, silent but alert.

"I'll repeat the question. In your professional opinion, Dr. Easton, is Missy strong enough to do this?"

"That, only Missy knows. I think personally it would be good for her. She wants to contribute, and she has experience. I also have to trust that if she decided she couldn't handle it, she would speak up." She looked at Missy, who nodded in affirmation.

"She'll never know if she doesn't try, Marcus. It might help her move forward." She paused, glancing at our clasped hands. "It might help you move forward."

I turned to Missy, who was watching me with anxious eyes.

"If I agree, you promise to tell me if it's too much?"

"Yes."

"And you'll work within the boundaries I set?"

"As long as they're fair. Don't give me a bunch of BS to do just to keep me off your back."

She was smart, but I grudgingly agreed.

"Okay, I'll get Damien to set you up in the apartment."

"I can't be in the command room?"

I shut my eyes, trying to find my patience. "I would prefer not. It's not only your case we're working on."

"Maybe on occasion?" She pushed.

I nodded tersely.

"Okay."

"And you keep seeing Dr. Easton."

"I planned to."

I looked at Dr. Easton. "Accommodating enough for you?"

A smile broke through her professional mask. "It's a start, Marcus."

Jesus. God save me from strong-minded women.

MISSY

I sat back, the hair on my forehead lifting with my long exhale of air. My days had taken on a semblance of order, one which helped me settle, yet still felt as if they weren't busy enough. As if I wasn't doing *enough* to help.

Marcus had Damien set me up with a laptop. It was incredibly fast and the software unlike anything I had used before now. Damien spent some time with me showing me how to use it, explaining the safeguards and encryption techniques. There was no camera on the laptop, and it was, as he assured me, completely untraceable. I spent hours poring over documents, files, and intel they had on various cases—some past, some ongoing—trying to find traces of the elusive Xander in them. Wanting, needing to know how I came into the picture.

Twice a week, I went for counseling. Dr. Easton had helped me a great deal. Marcus was right. It was easier to talk to her, knowing whatever I said was listened to and treated objectively. She was empathetic, but not involved. She helped me sort out some of my anger and worry.

Marcus had enough of both on his plate all the time. He took his role as leader very seriously. He constantly looked out for his men, ever vigilant with their safety. He was well respected by everyone on his team, and I knew Julian thought highly of him. He worked as hard, if not harder, always looking ahead, wanting to rid the world of as much darkness as possible. He was driven, strong, and determined.

I saw a different side of him. When we were alone, there was a teasing, softer side to him that he allowed me to see. He loved to cook, to putter in his little garden plot, to listen to music, and enjoy a glass of wine. He was infinitely tender, always just this side of rough— demanding, sweet, dirty, and loving. All of it rolled into his sexy body and killer looks. I never knew which Marcus would come out to play. Sometimes the evenings were long hours of talk and foreplay, followed by passion and lovemaking. Others were short and fast, the dark look in his eyes letting me know he would be fucking me hard and fast at any moment.

Yet even when he was at his most demanding—intense and dark—he never frightened me. His touch was never anything but perfect, he handled me carefully, and I knew I was safe. It allowed me to let go with him and explore him and us with an ease that surprised me. He made me feel comfortable enough to be Missy. I had asked Dr. Easton if something was wrong with me.

"I don't understand," she said with a frown.

"With what I went through, what I saw, the knowledge I have been exposed to—" I blew out a long breath "—shouldn't I be more, ah, reticent of sex?"

"Of sex, or of sex with Marcus?"

I felt my cheeks flame. "Yes," I mumbled.

She shook her head. "You went through a great deal. Something like that would have an effect on anyone. The fact that you are able to be free with Marcus, to enjoy sex, to embrace the passion he brings out in you, is a wonderful thing. You share something, and you should absolutely rejoice in the fact that he makes you feel safe enough to enjoy it."

She tapped on her notebook. "Don't kid yourself, though. You suffer in other ways, Missy. That's why you're here. Your experience has left its mark on you. But as for sex—enjoy it. Explore it."

I sighed as I returned to the present and looked at the piles of paper I had gone through. The door to the apartment was opened, and Marcus strode in, his gaze immediately finding me.

"Lunchtime," he stated.

I tried not to roll my eyes at him but failed. One way Marcus showed his care was by feeding me. I had gained back some of the weight I had lost, and I was stronger every day. After counseling, I used the gym in the building where Julian ran the team. Marcus introduced me to one of the trainers, and I worked with Ellen, building my strength and muscles. I had missed that part of my daily routine. I used to work out at the station all the time, and I had taken kickboxing lessons and had started looking into some martial arts training. For now, though, I was happy to be building my body back up, and I used Marcus's little room on the days I worked from here.

I picked up the sandwich he slid in front of me. "I can make my own lunch, you know." I wasn't much of a cook, but I could handle a sandwich. I made a mean pot roast, and my pancakes were pretty stellar. Marcus hadn't let me show him either, though.

"I know, but I like making you lunch." He grinned and bit into his much larger sandwich, chewing and swallowing before lifting his glass to his full mouth and taking a long drink of his water. He became serious, meeting my eyes across the table. "We have another tip. Once we confirm it, we're going to move fast."

"You've had a lot of them."

He ate for a moment in silence, nodding in acknowledgment.

"You think they are all Xander?"

"Same MO. Abandoned building, young women under twenty, small groups, easily moved, held in one place for a bit, then taken elsewhere."

"Do you think you'll find any, ah, like me?"

The last two raids, they had noticed several of the women bore a physical resemblance to me. None had been separated the way I was, but some of the women told them they had been put in front of a camera and dismissed.

"If so, we'll know it's him for sure." He reached across the table, flipping over his hand and waiting until I slid mine into his, then closing his fingers around my palm. "We'll figure this out, Missy. You're safe here. He isn't looking for you."

"But you think he's looking for someone like me."

He pushed away his empty plate. "Yes. My gut tells me so. I just don't know why." He dragged his hands through his hair. "We can't find him—he's like a ghost. One grainy picture. Lots of gossip and rumors. Even the assholes that work for him have no idea who he is or what he looks like. I don't know what drives him, what he's looking for."

"Maybe if you stopped killing the men who work for him, you could find out," I replied, lifting one eyebrow.

He shook his head. "We didn't kill anyone the last two raids. They were questioned, promised a new life, anything to get a handle on this fucker. We went through everything. He's good—too good at being elusive."

"And where are they now?"

It was his turn to lift an eyebrow. "We finished questioning them. They outlived their usefulness."

I knew what that meant, and I didn't respond. Marcus and his team meted out punishment and justice in their own way. I knew as well as they did, if they were let go, the men would simply return to their illegal pursuits.

"I wish I could help more. Remember more." Something was on the fringe of my memories.

Something small but significant. But the more I tried to recall it, the more it faded away.

"You're doing great, sweetheart. Damien says you made a few suggestions he's running down."

I pushed away my plate, my appetite gone. "Doesn't feel like enough."

"Is that all you're going to eat? Half a sandwich?"

"Yes." I paused. "I want to talk to Damien. Can I go down with you after lunch?"

He disliked me down in the command center. I knew he worried about the things I would see and hear, but I liked being down there. I was actually able to tune out most of the background noise and concentrate on the files I was working on. It was the energy, the buzz around me, that helped me focus. Up here, there was too much silence. Too much distance from where Marcus was. I felt better being in the same room with him, even if I couldn't touch him.

"Eat your sandwich, and you can come with me." He bargained.

"Make me pasta later, and I will," I countered.

"Fine."

"That angel-hair with the lemon cream sauce?" I asked hopefully.

He smiled, leaning forward and tucking a strand of hair behind my ear. "Whatever you want, sweetheart."

I picked up the sandwich, not letting him know I would eat it simply because he asked, even if he didn't make me pasta.

I didn't want him to know just how strong his power over me was.

The next day, I followed him down the stairs, staying close. At the door, I focused my attention on his fingers, watching carefully as he keyed in the numbers.

In the command room, I sat and talked to Damien, half listening as Marcus, Egan, Leo, and two other members of the team plotted out the next takedown. I didn't know them as well, but they seemed proficient and intelligent. As with all the team, they had an air of intensity about them.

"We're one hundred percent?" Marcus asked. "Certain of all of it?"

"Yes."

"We have the building bugged. I heard some chatter—they're expecting a few more 'packages' tonight. The last 'shipment,' they called it," Leo said with a grimace.

"Okay, so we go tomorrow." He glanced at Egan. "Everything ready?"

"You know it. In and out, save the day, then bye, bye, bye."

Marcus narrowed his eyes in my direction, and I dropped my head down, focusing on the paper in front of me. I hated it when he left. I knew the dangers he faced. I saw the guns and weapons these people kept. How dangerous they were. From the moment he left until he walked back in the door, I paced and worried. Sofia was there, or he left one of his men to watch over me, but it didn't help. His team were professionals. They knew what to do, when to do it, and how to come out of the missions alive and, most times, unhurt. But the wild card factor of not knowing how prepared the enemy was always lingered. The thought of him hurt, or worse, terrified me.

I looked up to see him watching me with an understanding look on his face. He crossed the room, standing behind me, his hand resting on my shoulder.

"Nice doodles."

The page was covered in my scribbles. He chuckled. "Still thinking of that silly movie you watched last night?"

I had sketched out the word Xanadu, using the same font the movie title was made from. I added a pair of skates and some hearts in my squiggles. I had to join in his amusement. "I guess so." I tended to doodle mindlessly when upset. "It's a classic," I argued.

"Classic shit," he mumbled.

Damien chuckled. "You're right on that one."

Marcus squeezed my shoulder. "Got everything you need?"

That was his way of telling me it was time to go. With a sigh, I stood. "Thanks, Damien."

"No problem." He handed me a list. "Here are some other places to check."

I nodded, taking the list and scanning it. The internet had two faces—the side most people saw, social media, helpful sites, information, great technology. The other side—the dark one, was enough to make your skin crawl. I shifted through so much horror and saw the worst of mankind's atrocious behavior as I tried to find hints of this Xander to help Marcus and his team. Every day, I understood Marcus's passion a little more, as well as his desire to protect me from all of it.

I gathered up my files and left. I headed upstairs, my footsteps heavy. In the apartment, I stared out at the city below, looking at the people coming and going, busy with their lives. Unseeing of the horrors that were all around them. Unconscious of the pain and strife many lived with.

I leaned my head on the glass, wishing I had never had to know about either.

I startled when Marcus appeared behind me, wrapping his arms around my waist and drawing me back to his chest. He met my eyes in the reflection in the glass.

"Too much today, sweetheart?"

I nodded, unable to speak.

"That's enough for now."

"You're going tomorrow?"

He turned me in his embrace, holding me close. He tilted up my chin and dropped a kiss to my mouth. "I'll be home tomorrow as well. We have this."

"I hate it," I whispered. "I hate the feeling when you walk out that door and I know you're facing danger."

He stroked my cheek. "I'm not used to someone worrying about me."

I covered his hand, turning my head and kissing the palm. "I do."

He bent, brushing a kiss to my lips, his lingering. "I'll be fine. Do you know why?"

"Because you're a professional?"

He chuckled low. "Yes. Plus, I know you're here. Waiting for me."

With a whimper, I flung my arms around his neck, pulling him down to my mouth. He tugged me to his chest, his kiss firm and claiming. Deep and carnal.

Sweeping away any and all thoughts except those of him. Us.

That was what I wanted. Needed right now.

He lifted me, and I wrapped my legs around his waist. He kept our mouths molded together as he walked down the hall, his steps sure and fast.

In his room, he followed me down to the mattress, his weight pressing me deep into the bed. "Tell me what you want," he demanded, dragging his mouth to my ear.

"Make me forget everything but you, Marcus. Make me yours all over again."

"Hold tight," he murmured, his dark eyes glittering in the light. "I'm going to rock your world."

"I'm counting on it."

CHAPTER TEN

Missy

Darkness surrounded the city, the streetlights bright down below. I stared out the window of the apartment, restless and edgy. Marcus had been gone for hours. The building felt empty even though I knew Sofia was in her place, one of Marcus's men was outside the door, and a couple people were still working in the command center.

Marcus hadn't been pleased when I'd shown up in the room earlier this morning. He'd come out of his office frowning when he saw me sitting with Egan. He crossed the room to my side.

"What are you doing?"

"Egan is showing me how he designs the charges. It's fascinating."

He regarded me with ill-concealed impatience. "I'm not happy about that, but I meant how did you get in here? I left you upstairs."

"I came in like everyone else. Through the door. I can't ghost through objects, Marcus."

He leaned down, his mouth close to my ear. "How did you get the passcode for the door?"

"I memorized it yesterday," I responded, keeping my eyes on the computer screen Egan was using.

"Damien, change the code," he barked, straightening up, taking my arm.

I didn't respond and let him lead me upstairs. "You don't need to know about explosives," he snapped, sitting me on the sofa. "Do your research."

I waited a bit, then headed back down, taking my laptop and sliding into a corner in the room. I worked for a while, the sounds of the busy room helping me to focus. When Marcus appeared again, his tone exasperated, I tried not to laugh.

"Why are you never where I leave you? How the hell did you get in this time?"

"I called Julian and asked for permission. He gave me a code."

Marcus walked into his office, slamming the door. I heard some yelling on a one-sided conversation, then he came back out.

"Missy. My office. Now."

Egan looked over with a comical grin. "Good luck," he muttered. "I know that tone."

So did I. But I marched into Marcus's office and sat down. "Yes, sir?"

"Don't play coy with me. I want you upstairs."

"I want to be here."

"Why are you being so stubborn?"

"Because I feel better when I'm here. I'm close to you, and the background noise helps me concentrate. Upstairs, there is too much silence. It bothers me."

That took away his anger, and his shoulders slumped in defeat.

"No explosive lessons. And don't touch the weapons. Stay in the corner."

"Anything else, Dad?"

He glared at me, and I grinned.

"You interfere, and you're out."

I jumped to my feet. "Got it." I hurried out of his office before he could add any other stupid rules I would have to ignore.

I did leave the space once they got down to the mission for the night. He felt better with my not knowing, and I could respect that. Now that he was gone, I had no desire to go downstairs.

I sat down, pulling my laptop onto my knees and studying the notes I had made. I was missing something. We were all missing something.

A smile played on my face as I saw how Egan had scribbled a Z over the X of Xanadu. *"It makes no sense how something spelled with an X and a Z can be pronounced the same way. It should be X-anadu. Like X-ray," he stated, his Romanian accent thick. "Your English is too confusing."*

I had laughed and ignored him. But as I looked at his scribble, something niggled again at my tired brain. The beginning of an idea formed. Something so simple, it perhaps was overlooked. Or maybe it had been thought of and nothing came of it. Either way, I wanted to check it out, but I needed to be able to concentrate. To think it through carefully and decide how to go about it the best way. When I heard the low ping of the elevator, I shut the laptop. I would start in the morning.

MARCUS

My body was weary as I headed down the hall. My mind was not. It was full of the terrified faces of the women we had pulled out of the dark, damp cellar of an old house. Something had tugged at me, and it wasn't until Damien said something that the troublesome thought congealed in my mind.

"These women all look like Missy. Every one of them."

He was right. That coincidence had been growing. They were similar in coloring and size. None of them had the unique eyes or were as tiny as she was, but the resemblance was there. Obviously, this asshole we were chasing now had an image in his mind. He was dealing in a *type*.

139

I didn't like it. I wanted to know why, and I wanted to know who.

And I wanted to stop him.

Preferably with a bullet between his eyes.

I didn't make it to my door before it was yanked open and Missy stood in the doorway, looking anxious and jittery.

"Sweetheart," I said, forcing my feet to go faster to reach her. "What's wrong? Did something happen?"

She flung herself into my arms, her grip tight. "I was so worried. You were gone so long."

I carried her into the apartment and shut the door, her sweet words on echo in my head. I wasn't used to anyone worrying about me, but it warmed my heart to hear those words. I walked over to the sofa and sat heavily.

She lifted her head, and I brushed the hair back from her face. The bruises were mostly gone, although some faint shadows still remained. Her lovely moss-green eyes were darker than usual—more gray—indicating her anxiety. I pressed a kiss to her forehead, the tender gesture still new and unfamiliar to me.

"It was tricky and took longer. We were in a residential area, so we had to be cautious."

"Was there a gas leak?" she asked, knowing how we covered up the reason for the demolished buildings.

"There will be tomorrow. We didn't want to do it in the middle of the night. Egan and Damien will be there tomorrow to check it out and flip the switch. Make sure no one is hurt."

"Did you get the, ah, people in charge?"

I scratched my chin. "The last two were different. Fewer girls, only guards."

She frowned. "Why is that, do you think?"

"I have to figure that out. Something's changed."

"You look exhausted."

I met her worried gaze, running my finger down her cheek. "It takes a little out of me every time we do this. The images stay clearer longer. I feel the fear and anxiety of the victims more. It lingers. It drains me," I admitted. "Especially—" I stopped speaking.

"Since me?" she asked knowingly.

"Yes. I see you in every one of them. The fear, the pain, the terror."

"What about the hope? The relief when they realize you're there to help not hurt? The gratitude?"

She was right. It was there as well. The grateful tears, the sobs of relief. The whispers of thanks and the clutch of their fingers when they accepted our help to get them from the darkness.

"I was never more grateful for anything in my life," Missy murmured. "You were like a hero, reaching into that cage and freeing me. Wrapping me in a warm blanket and holding me. I went from being deathly frightened to safe." She stroked my cheek. "I had never known such safety until your arms, Marcus."

"You will always be safe with me."

"I know."

I stood, carrying her to the bathroom, setting her on the vanity. I shrugged out of my shirt and pants and helped her off with her clothes. I carried her into the shower, letting the hot spray cleanse my body and ease my tension. She insisted on washing me, her hands soft and soothing, helping me relax. Once I had rinsed off, I picked her up again, taking her to my large bed and sitting on the edge. I grabbed a condom, and she straddled me, her heat and wetness open to my cock. Our mouths fused together, and I slipped inside, groaning at the feel of her. We moved slowly, building a fire that burned low and hot. She caressed me with her hands, stroking and gentle. Her body was a panacea, easing my anxiety, taking me away from the darkness, and surrounding me with her light. I held her tight as she climaxed, her orgasm triggering mine, and I fell with her, clutching her close and moaning her name.

After, we lay in each other's arms, relaxed and sated. Strangely, in my head, I saw the grateful looks, the relief, and the thankfulness from the women earlier. I was able to concentrate on that rather than the darkness that started it all.

I pressed a kiss to Missy's head in an unspoken thank-you. She sighed and fell asleep—me not far behind her.

The next afternoon, I was in the command center, staring at the files in front of me.

"Something's changed," I griped. "What the fuck has changed?"

"He's becoming sloppy," Damien agreed.

"No, it's more than that. What you said last night about them looking like Missy. You're right. All the women in the last two raids have had her coloring. I don't think it's a coincidence."

"That was only the last two. Could be a fluke. The raid before that there was a—" he waved his hand as he searched for the word "—variety."

"I think those women had been locked up as long as Missy had. These were shorter time frames. Something has set him off."

Julian spoke up. "Are you sure it's him—this Xander scum?"

I nodded. "It's him—it's definitely him. It's like he's—" I shook my head "—I don't know what, but I don't like it."

Julian studied the table, the documents, maps, and lists we had laid out. He frowned. "I agree. Something is up. What changed recently?"

The room was quiet for a moment, then a voice I shouldn't be hearing in this room spoke up.

"You took me."

I whirled around. "Just because you have the passcode for the stairs, you aren't supposed to roam the building. Get out."

Missy crossed her arms. "No. I can help with this."

I didn't want her to hear this. I knew it would upset her. "You're already helping. Your computer work is helping a lot." I pointed to the door. "You know the way back upstairs. Find it."

She tossed her hair in a defiant gesture I had come to know well. Too well. "No, I think I'm good here."

Julian spoke. "Marcus, back down. Maybe Melissa has a different perspective."

I swung around to tell him off, but he was standing, his hands on the table, frowning, in full commander mode. I knew I was being overridden.

Missy sat down across from me. She was pale and intense-looking. My anger eased off, and I stopped shooting her glares because I could tell she had come down here with a purpose that wasn't just to piss me off. Her hand gripped a file so tight, her knuckles were white.

"What did you find?"

"I found him," she stated simply.

"What?"

"I found Xander."

Now she had all our attention.

"How?" I demanded.

"His real name is spelled with a Z, not an X. He swapped it out with the first initial of his first name. I am sure he thinks it's clever."

"This isn't some fucking game."

"It is to him. He's—" she shivered "—he's horrible."

"Tell us," Julian said.

"Xavier Zander. Age thirty. Only surviving family member of the Zander family. His parents were murdered. His sister committed suicide."

"Murdered?"

She nodded. "If I'm right, by him, I think."

"Jesus. And his sister?"

She pulled out a photo and slid it my way. I picked it up, shock making my eyes go wide. I met her anxious gaze. "You look just like her."

She nodded. "My eyes are grayer, but you would only see that in person. I am almost identical."

I handed the photo to Julian, who studied it, then handed it on to Damien and Egan. Leo got up and strolled over, whistling low under his breath.

"Mystery solved," he murmured.

"What is your theory?" I asked.

"I found an old profile on social media. His sister's. She mentioned him in some of her posts. I think she had more than one account, but this was the only one I could find. Then I went to the dark web. That's how I found him. He was, ah, in love with his sister. Obsessed. He didn't try to hide it. He had all sorts of posts about her—before and after she died. I think his parents tried to interfere, and he murdered them. His sister killed herself not long after."

"I assume she didn't share his feelings?"

"I don't think so."

"So, what?" I growled. "He's trying to replace her?"

"Yes. I went through a bunch of the reports. How often the missing women had similar coloring to mine." She paused and swallowed. "Why he got so excited when he saw me. I look like her. I'm almost identical. That's why he told my capturers good job and why I was put in the cage." She leaned on the table. "There was something in my mind, something I couldn't remember. When I was in front of the camera, the man—this Xavier—said something. One word, but it sounded like an endearment. But it wasn't—it was her name. He whispered 'Xyla'—almost as if it was a blessing."

"That's why you were the only one taken that night," Julian mused. "Why none of the other women reported missing were with you in that group."

"Yes. I was transported here for him specifically." She drew in a long breath. "I know Zander is into selling women. But he keeps his eyes open to replace his dead sister he was consumed with," Missy said. "I was kept aside for him."

"Wouldn't you be given deferential treatment, then?" Leo asked. "If you were so special?"

"No. That was part of his plan," she murmured.

"She's right," I said, seeing where Missy was taking this. "She would be treated terribly, so when she was given to Zander, his treatment of her would seem like a gift." I studied Missy, who was nodding. "Perfect Stockholm syndrome. He gets a look-alike to fulfill his sick fantasies, and the girl has no idea."

"Until she's of no use anymore." Missy finished. "Then it starts all over again."

"We have to stop him. That twisted bastard," I snarled, pushing up from the table.

"We're still missing something," Julian mused. "We need to figure out what we're missing."

I heard a lot of mutterings behind me, and I had to inhale some long breaths in order to calm down. The thought of how close that revolting bastard had come to getting his hands on Missy. What he would have done to her if he had— I couldn't stomach the possibilities of the hell her life would have been. How quickly it would have been over for her.

"He was—is—obsessed with her. It's as if he thinks she is still alive somehow. His posts were disturbing before she died. After, they became—" she shivered "—unnerving. He will never stop looking. Feeding his fixation. Searching for his 'perfection.' His Xyla."

"How did she die?"

"She threw herself off a bridge. They never found the body, which has only fed into his delusion."

"We need a new plan," Julian said. "We need to flush him out. Instead of burning down his buildings, he needs to come to us."

"How?" Damien asked.

"You use me as a decoy," Missy said calmly.

I was aghast at her suggestion. "I am stopping this shit right now." I leaned on the table, glaring at her. "Don't even fucking go there."

She didn't react. "It would work."

"He thinks you're dead. It's going to stay that way."

"Then make me undead. Use whatever you use to let it slip a lone survivor was found and show my picture so he would see it. Set me up somewhere easy for him to get to. Say I have total memory loss. You could lure him."

"To what end? So you end up back in another cage? Do you know what you're asking? What horrors you're risking?"

She stood, her anger now matching mine. "No, you wouldn't let that happen. Embed a chip in me—a dozen if you want. I'll keep a weapon hidden."

"You gonna shove a gun up your ass?" I asked sarcastically. "Because they'll strip you totally, and you'll be fucked again."

"No, I'll hide a blade somewhere. They never touched my hair last time. I could weave one in."

"A knife?" I spat. "You think you could defend yourself with a knife? I doubt you can even cut bread without hurting yourself. Give it up, little girl. You aren't playing with the big boys. And we're not using you. End of story."

I strode to the cupboard, grabbing a cup. There was a sound, high and fast, and I felt the heat of something pass by my face. The collective inhale me from behind was startling, and I stared at the door beside me and the small knife Damien had been using earlier to peel an apple that was now embedded in the wood, the handle quivering from the force of its trajectory. I turned and met Missy's furious gaze.

"I think I've proven my point, *big boy*." Her voice dropped to a frigid level. "I *am* here to play, so get over yourself, asshole."

The slam of the door echoed in the room.

I stared at the door, shock rendering me useless for a minute. Then I was racing after Missy. Julian stood, holding up his hand.

"Marcus."

"Not right now."

He shook his head. "Following her is not a good idea."

I brushed past him. "I have to."

"Then you need to listen to her."

"No, *you* need to mind your own fucking business."

"Watch your mouth," he warned.

"Sorry, Commander," I snarled. "I am talking her out of this stupid idea, and no one is going to say a word about it to me."

He sat down, shaking his head. "I'll be here."

I caught the last few words as the door shut behind me.

"If there's anything left of you."

———

I pounded up the stairs, my feet sounding like a herd of elephants. Fury rippled under my skin at her words and actions. Another quarter of an inch and that knife would have been buried in my cheek. She was careless and acting like a child. And if she thought I would actually agree to allow her to be involved in this case again, offering herself up as a sacrifice, she was more delusional than I thought.

She was not going to be put at risk. Period.

I was so angry I had to punch in my code three times to open the door. I expected to find Missy standing in the living room, hands on her hips, ready to fight. Instead, only silence greeted me. For an instant, my anger was replaced with worry, and I wondered if she had somehow left. Except I heard a sound down the hall and knew she was in the bedroom.

No doubt sulking.

I stalked down the hall and threw open the door, ready in case she had another fucking knife in her hand. Something akin to shock hit me when I saw my suitcase on the bed and an angry Missy shoving the clothing I had bought her into it. Ice wrapped around my chest.

I shut the door behind me loudly, leaning against it.

"Going somewhere?" I asked, sarcasm dripping from every word.

"Anywhere you're not," she snapped, walking past me and grabbing a few more things.

"Need cab fare?"

She lifted her head, her gaze frosty and cold. "No. Julian will take me to a safe house. He has already assured me of that. Then he'll help me get home once we are finished with this case."

Shock rendered me immobile and speechless.

Julian?

When had he told her that?

"You're not fucking leaving. And you're not getting involved with this case again."

She slammed the lid of the suitcase shut. "Yes, I fucking am."

I stalked toward her. "If you think I am letting you go out there half-cocked, with some crazy idea about this investigation—"

She cut me off. "You're the one going off half-cocked, Marcus. What I do or not do is none of your concern anymore."

I grabbed her shoulders. "You *are* my fucking concern."

She shook her head wildly. "No, I am not."

"What did you think you were proving down there with that little knife stunt? You're lucky I hadn't turned my head! Did you think about that?" My hands tightened on her arms. "Or did you want to hurt me?"

"No, I didn't." She broke out of my hold, pushing me away. "I'm an expert with a knife, Marcus. I can calculate the speed, angle, and trajectory to throw it and hit—or, in your case—*not* hit my target every single damn time. I was so good, they had me show off my skills at the academy." She jabbed me in the chest. "If you would ever talk to me about my life, you'd know that, but you just made me realize all I am is something for you to pity and play with."

I blinked. *That was what she thought?*

"I know I'm a rookie, but I'm smart. I might be at the start of my career and learning, but I learn fast."

"And yet you ended up in that cage," I said.

I deserved the slap I got for that remark. Her hand lifted and swung in a perfect arc, and I knew it was coming. I didn't try to duck. I met her wide eyes as the sound of her palm on my face echoed in the room. My cheek stung from the impact, and my eyes watered with the force of her anger.

"You know that wasn't my fault. I did everything right," she whispered.

I did know that, but I didn't back down. My anger was out of control.

"Did that feel good?" I asked, my voice low. "You want to hit me again? Throw another knife at me and not miss this time? You want to take out your frustrations on me? You know you can't cut it in this career, but you're determined to try—even if you end up dead."

"I hate you," she snarled, pushing at my chest. "You insufferable, egotistical—" a sob escaped her mouth "—asshole."

"What are you trying to do?" I gritted out through clenched teeth. "Why are you insisting on trying to offer yourself up as a sacrifice? What the hell are you trying to prove?"

"That I can do it!" she yelled, almost panting. "I am not going to let him beat me! I can help. I want to help, and you keep stopping me! You won't even listen with an open mind, you stupid, arrogant *jerk*."

My fear and worry escaped at her words. I shook my head.

"Don't ask me to do that, sweetheart." My voice broke, and she stopped her hand waving and stared at me.

"Don't ask me to risk you ending up caged and taken away. To be hurt so badly I can't help you heal." I met her confused gaze. "I can't."

For a moment, there was only the sound of our ragged breathing. Then suddenly, she lunged, locking her arms around my neck, crashing her mouth to mine. I was right there with her, dragging her body up my torso, wrapping her legs around my waist. Our tongues dueled and fought for dominance, neither of us giving an inch. She bit my bottom lip, and I tasted blood, ignoring it and kissing her harder, grinding her lips against her teeth. She clutched the back of my hair, yanking, and I hissed in pain. Turning, I pressed her to the door, trapping her between the hard wood and my body. I reached between us, tearing her shirt, the material rending easily with my fists. I yanked down her lacy bra, her breasts spilling over the top. I sucked hard at her nipples, biting and squeezing them until they were red and abraded from my mouth. She clawed at my neck and shoulders, hissing like a kitten between her groans and whimpers. I walked backward, then turned and dropped her on the mattress, tearing off her yoga pants and underwear, and pulling my shirt over my head. I stared at her, her legs scissoring, her face flushed.

"Tell me you want this. Tell me—"

"Shut up and fuck me, Marcus."

I kicked off my jeans and fell on top of her, pinning her down, my weight causing us to sink into the thick bed. I pushed open her legs and slammed into her. She cried out, her back arching, her orgasm catching us both off guard. I rode it out, thrusting into her, tossing her legs over my shoulders, and circling my hips fast and hard. Sweat beaded on my forehead, covering my back. I hovered over her, our eyes locked. Hate and anger burned and morphed into passion and need. Her body softened, and she lifted her arms, cupping my face, and stroking over my skin. I stopped and bent, covering her mouth with mine, this time our exchange slow and languid. Passionate and deep. Warm, wet, and aching in its need. I slipped my arms under her, pulling her close, and moved again. Long, unhurried glides of my hips. Deep, soul-shattering kisses. Dragging, leisurely caresses over our bodies. Murmurs of passion, apology, and need. My orgasm was a slow-building glow inside me. My balls tightened, and my body lit up as tendrils of ecstasy built and exploded, the flames so hot I was certain I would be reduced to ash when it was done. Missy met my passion, her second orgasm making her shake and quiver, gasp my name, and clutch me deep inside her, stretching my pleasure into uncharted territory I didn't want to discover the way back from.

I fucked her until I was empty and aching. My body stilled with exhaustion. Sated beyond anything I had known before.

And she lay under me, still, quiet, and crying.

I lifted my head, horrified. "I hurt you?"

"No, that was just so…powerful."

156

I ran a finger over her cheek, tracing her swollen lips. "It was."

Our gazes locked again. I tried desperately to explain. To make her understand. "I can't let you risk yourself. If I fail and you're taken, I—"

She touched my mouth with her fingers. "You won't let that happen, Marcus. You come up with a plan, and I promise I'll stick to it. You'll have your team. I'll have you. We'll get him."

I dropped my head. "You shouldn't trust me so much."

She slipped her hand under my chin, lifting my face. "But I do. I trust you more than anything or anyone —ever."

I searched her eyes. "Why?"

"Because—" She swallowed. "Because I love you."

Those three little words were like gunshots to my heart. They drove into me with so much power, they embedded themselves into my soul forever. I pulled her up tight to my chest, kissing her forehead.

"I love you, sweetheart. So much I fear what will happen if I fuck this up. I will never forgive myself. I will never get over it."

She drew back and cupped my face, her fingers drawing restless circles on my skin. "You love me?"

"Yes. And I was a jerk earlier. I was so scared that I lashed out." A dry chuckle escaped my lips. "And your little trick with the knife was pretty spectacular. Which pissed me off as much as it impressed me."

She sighed. "Do you remember when you told me about Damien? How you saw something in him and you helped him discover his potential?"

I frowned. "Yes."

"And you trust him?"

"Completely."

"Talk to *me*, Marcus. Find *my* potential. Trust *me*." She swallowed. "I think-I think, together, we can do this."

My heart thumped rapidly in my chest.

"If I'm brave enough to do this," she whispered, "then you need to be brave enough to let me." She gripped my shoulders. "If I don't help stop him, I will never be free, Marcus. He'll always be there, you'll always wonder if he'll find me. See me accidentally and take me away. We will never have any peace. You have to let me help you end him. There is no choice here. You have to see that."

I gave in. She was right—I had no choice. She wasn't going to let this go, and it was obvious I needed to figure out how to approach this horrendous task so her risk was minimal.

"We'll go talk to Julian," I said.

"I need to clean up."

I began to move, then froze. "I didn't wear a condom."

"I'll ask Sofia about the morning-after pill and getting on birth control."

"I'm sorry. I was carried away."

"I know—me too." Her smile was shy. "That was my first make-up sex."

"Ah, I'd call that angry sex, sweetheart. At least, at the beginning."

"Oh. There's a difference?"

I bent close. "I can show you make-up sex if you want."

She arched an eyebrow. "Again?"

My mouth hovered over hers. "Again."

"Okay then, big boy. Apologize. I expect it to be good."

"And I'll deliver."

"Good."

CHAPTER ELEVEN

Marcus

We headed back to the command center, not surprised to find Julian still there. He was flipping through the files Missy had compiled as well as scanning two computer screens, typing quickly. He didn't say anything until we sat down. I sipped a cup of coffee, waiting. I knew he had to speak first.

"Have you cleared the air?" he asked, not looking up. "Come to an agreement?"

"Yes," I replied.

"Good." He lifted his head, his expression tolerant but serious. "I don't want to know all the details, but good. We can move on now? Figure this shit out?"

"Yes," I repeated. "And I apologize for my disrespect. I was, ah, upset."

He shook his head with a grimace. "You're worse than Matteo."

"Evie never wanted to take down a bad guy."

He smirked, one corner of his mouth lifting higher than the other. "Yet, she did."

I blinked, realizing he was right. Evie had been instrumental in taking out Raoul Carmen. She had been brave and inventive, giving us the time to arrive and kill him. And she did it with no training or preplanning. None of us knew he was even alive until he showed up, threatening her life. I had been with Matteo that day and witnessed her resourcefulness myself.

"True."

"I understand your worries, Marcus, but Missy is right. She's the key here. And no matter how you feel, she *is* involved. She's more involved than anyone, given what she has already been through."

"I can't let that happen again."

Julian blew out a long breath. "You're going to have to. The only way to trap him is to let him have her."

The growl that split the air was almost inhuman, and I had no recollection of it coming from my mouth. The next thing I knew, I had Julian's shirt twisted in my hand and him pulled out of his chair as I snarled in his face. Missy tugged on my arm, her voice frantic.

"Calm down, Marcus!"

Julian met my furious gaze, his calm and even. "I suggest you do as she says, or I'll pull you off this case and you'll have zero input."

I released his shirt and sat down, shocked. "Jesus, Julian, I'm sorry," I rasped, leaning my elbows on my knees and dropping my head into my hands. "I don't know what happened."

"I do," he said patiently. "But you need to rein it in, Marcus. Put aside your personal fears and concentrate on what we need to do to keep Missy safe, end this scumbag, and get on with your life."

"But we have to use her to get him," I said, lifting my head, sounding weary.

"Yes. But if Evie can help with no training, imagine what your little knife thrower here can do." He winked at Missy. "Impressive, by the way."

She dipped her chin in acknowledgment, her anxious gaze on me. I pulled her hand to my chest and ghosted a kiss to her knuckles.

"It's okay, sweetheart. I'm calm."

"For how long?"

"Until this is over. Until he is dead." I had to be, because there was no other option. I needed a clear head to protect her.

I had to ask a question, though. "How *did* you learn to throw a knife like that? It's not a course taught at the academy."

"No. Where I lived growing up, there wasn't much to do. There was a boy on my street who liked knives. He did target practice every day after school. He was a bit of a loner like me. We got to be friends, and he taught me to throw. I loved it. And I was good. I self-taught myself everything he couldn't show me." She shrugged. "I had a lot of time on my hands and lots of empty fields and trees to practice on."

I leaned closer. "How good a friend?" I growled lowly.

She rolled her eyes. "A friend," she insisted. "I was a kid and a tomboy. Eventually, he moved with his family somewhere else." She shook her head. "Neanderthal," she muttered.

I ignored her. She was right, though. When it came to her, I was like a caveman.

She cleared her throat and returned to the subject at hand.

"What about my idea? Letting it slip I'm alive?" Missy asked.

Julian shook his head. "Too vague."

"He could miss it or assume it was someone else. I don't want to post your picture either," I added.

"But I think you're onto something, Missy. I'm certain someone on your team is in his pocket—it only makes sense. We're digging into bank records right now. I think you were set up."

"How do we use that to our advantage?" she asked.

"I'm certain it will be one of the head men. We contact whoever the leak is. In private. Tell him we found you before the building was destroyed. That you have no memory, but one of the other women we rescued knew your name and I traced you to him."

She furrowed her brow.

"And?"

"I'll tell him you need to be transported back to your home. You're well enough to travel, but I won't release you to anyone but your team."

"I'm still not seeing it," she said.

I turned toward her. "He'll contact Zander, Missy. Zander will send one of his men, and you'll be taken to him, not home. Since you have no memory, you would accept the person as trustworthy and not question where you're going. We would assume you were safe and be done with it."

"But you can track me?"

Julian nodded. "We have these new chips. Untraceable. Undetectable. Tiny enough, you can wear one in an earring. We'll weave a few in your hair. We can put a fake mole on your arm and hide it under that. We will *not* lose you. You get to Zander and lead us to him. We'll have an arsenal of firepower and men to get to you. We take him down and end this shit. You go home to Marcus and live your life."

"You make it sound easy," she murmured.

"It's not. We have to plan. Strategize. We'll be going in blind since we have no idea where you'll be taken."

"I think he's outside Montreal. I saw some pictures and did searches on them. The bridge his sister jumped from is on the St. Lawrence."

Julian smiled. "Good job. I did some checking while you were, ah, upstairs, *talking*, and I would agree. His parents held a fair amount of property he would have inherited. There is a lot of it—and some close to the water. When I checked the land titles, they are now held by a numbered company. All of them were sold just after they died. Most of their holdings were."

"That's when he went into hiding," I noted.

"Yes. His parents' deaths were ruled an accident, but I agree with Missy. I think he had a hand in it. His sister disappeared from the boarding school she was in, he disappeared from normal life—almost all traces of them were erased off social media." He smiled coldly. "Unless, of course, you know how to dig." He pushed some papers our way. "I found some other posts. Missy is right. He is beyond disturbed."

"And after he showed up on the dark web?"

"He was there before, but his presence became more noticeable. He became known as Mr. X. His anger was out of control, and it's only gotten worse."

"His sister suffered because of it," Missy said. "I think his mind fractured, and he became dangerous."

Julian hummed in agreement. "I have our team digging. A lot of shit is buried that we need to uncover before we move forward. We need to have everything at our disposal—get to know this sick fuck as well as we can, then move."

"And end him," I said.

"Yes. Once and for all. Dismantle all his holdings and find as many victims as possible."

"Agreed."

I felt the shiver that went through Missy. Despite her insistence and bravado, I knew she was terrified. I squeezed her hand and shifted closer.

I needed to be strong for both of us.

I prayed I was strong enough.

Zing!

I tried to shut out the never-ending sound across the room, but it was impossible. I turned in my chair, watching as Missy pulled a knife from somewhere on her body and tossed it, hitting the target every time. I had to admit, she was impressive. But most of the time, it didn't help ease my fears.

"Again," Allen instructed. Julian had brought him in, knowing his weapons training would give her the best shot. "I want you moving this time. There's a good chance you won't have the luxury to be in one spot when you're reaching for the blade. You need to grab it and throw in seconds. Split seconds."

Missy nodded, reconcealing the knife Allen had specially made for her. She practiced every day. Sat beside me as we pored over reports and maps. Dug up more intel on Xavier Zander. The more we dug, the darker it got. Yet she never reacted or showed any fear—at least when we were with the team.

At night when we were alone, it was a different story. I saw the pull of anxiety in her eyes. Watched her lose weight as her appetite waned. Noticed the deepening shadows under her eyes. When Julian commented on it, she had waved him off.

"If I show up healthy and well, it will set off Zander's suspicions. Supposedly I have been badly injured and have no memory. I need to look the part."

I doubted he was any more fooled by her words than I was.

Last night, she had barely slept at all, and I knew it was beginning to overwhelm her. The urge to spirit her away, to simply disappear, grew within me every day. I had never pictured my time with the organization coming to an end only a handful of years after I took over from Matteo. But I knew if we survived this, I needed to put her first. That meant either sending her away and continuing with this half-life, or walking away and finding a different life with Missy. Since I couldn't even imagine a future that no longer contained her, my choice was obvious. I was almost certain Julian already knew that. I was sure he wouldn't be far behind me. He had been doing this longer than I had and had already lost so much personally.

Last evening, I found Missy upstairs in the garden in the darkness, sitting and watching the stars. I stepped behind her, sitting down and pulling her back to my bare chest.

"What are you thinking?" I asked. "Be honest."

"I wonder, if things go wrong, if I'll ever see the stars again," she admitted.

"We can stop this. Find another way," I insisted.

"No. You need me to draw him out. He is so delusional, Marcus. When he finds out I'm alive, he'll be certain that he has found what he's been searching for."

I tightened my grip on her.

"You have to let me do this. Otherwise, I have to hide the rest of my life. And I'll resent that. I'll resent you. You'll start to hate me." She lifted her head. *"We won't last."*

"I could never hate you, sweetheart."

"You would if I were unhappy all the time. I can't be hidden away, Marcus. I'm not that sort of girl. I have to be able to live." She sighed. *"You can keep chasing him, shutting down his kidnapping rings, but he'll never stop. He'll find other women, other countries, even. Unless you end him, you'll never be done."* She wrapped her hands around mine. *"You have to give me to him. It will distract him, and you can move. He doesn't leave his estate, so you have to go to him, and I can help get you in."*

As much as I hated it, she was right about everything. The estate was a fortress. We had never seen anything like it. She was our Trojan horse. She would go in like a benevolent gift and open up hell once she was inside.

As long as everything went according to plan.

That was the one thing beyond our control. We had Plan A through to Plan Z, but there were still things that could go wrong.

And if they did, and she was put in more danger than she already was, I wasn't sure how I was going to cope. If he destroyed her, even if I managed to kill him, my life would never be the same. I would never be able to forgive myself, even if she did.

"I'm strong," she whispered, as if sensing my thoughts.

"I know you are."

"Not physically," she admitted. "That was what always kept me back. No matter how hard I worked, I was barely able to pass the physical part of the training. But mentally, I'm tough, Marcus. No matter what he does to me, I can handle it. You come and find me. I'll come back to you."

I turned her in my arms, yanking her tight to my chest, and covered her mouth with mine. I kissed her until we were both breathless. Almost panting in our desire and need for each other. I pulled the thin nightshirt she had on over her head, tossing it to the grass. She yanked at my sweats, freeing my aching cock. I lifted her so her legs straddled me, and I sank inside her, her heat surrounding me. We moved together, never separating, our skin flush and our mouths fused tight. She clutched my shoulders, her nails sinking into my skin, her low whimpers and moans music to my ears. I gripped her hips, tracing circles on her skin. I absorbed her taste, the feel of her in my arms. How she felt around my cock, how her body felt melded to mine. Her nipples were hard peaks on my skin, the skin on her back like silk under my fingers.

We moved and fucked, lost to each other, nothing else in the world mattering in that exact moment but her and me. Us.

Her head fell back and she stiffened, crying out my name into the night. I pulled her back to me, groaning out my release, grateful she'd had a shot two weeks ago and we no longer had to worry about birth control.

We sat in silence, our bodies wrapped around each other until she shivered in the cooling air. I stood and carried her back downstairs to our bed. We fell asleep wrapped up together, but neither of us rested well. We wouldn't until this was behind us.

Julian brought me out of my musings.

"I'm calling Dan Jared today."

My hand froze, my coffee cup partway to my mouth.

"Today?" I questioned. "Are we—is she ready?"

"Everything is set, Marcus. If much more time passes, it won't make any sense."

"And we're sure it's him?"

He nodded. "It took some digging, but Damien found an offshore account. He has a lot of money in there, and the dates line up. He's been doing this for a while. There was a huge deposit the night he handed Missy to Zander's men."

"Bastard."

"His record is spotless. Comes across as the nicest guy you'd want to meet. Well-liked by superiors and fellow officers. The last one you would suspect."

"Missy didn't like him," I pointed out. When Julian had shown her the evidence, she hadn't seemed surprised and admitted she never cared for him.

"There was something about him—something I didn't trust," she said. "He did all the right things, said all the right things, but he gave me the creeps."

"She has good instincts, which are going to help her right now," Julian stated. "You need to trust her."

"I do," I replied. I met his eyes. "I also love her, and the thought of her being even close to that lowlife makes me ill. Knowing he'll have her is killing me, Julian."

"I know. I realize that. But it has to happen. And we'll have her out as fast as possible. We'll know where she is. She'll be tracked. She'll have a weapon." Julian's expression was understanding but his voice firm. "She is ready. So are you—at least on one side. The truth is, you'll never be ready. So I have to make the decision, and tomorrow is the day."

I couldn't respond. I wanted to protest, but he was right.

"We have backups. Missy is smart and capable," he assured me.

I leaned forward, letting my fear and anger bleed through. "Unless she's locked in a cage. Or worse," I hissed.

"We're not going to let that happen, Marcus."

I sat back, the feeling in my chest heavy. Somehow, something in my gut told me it was out of our hands.

And I fucking hated that I was always right.

CHAPTER TWELVE

Missy

Marcus disappeared midafternoon, not saying a word. He had been quiet since talking to Julian in the morning, not even giving me shit when I sat with Egan, who explained the intricacies of designing and wiring a bomb. I had to admit I felt a bit disappointed Marcus wasn't there to stand over me, growling and snarling, ordering me upstairs and losing it when I refused. I sort of liked it when his dark eyes would snap fire and his sexy scowl came out. I also liked it when he slung me over his shoulder and carried me to where he wanted me like the caveman he was underneath the modern veneer. I always protested and demanded to be put down, but I liked how even when he was bristling like a porcupine, his hands were gentle and he always stroked my leg as he climbed the steps, muttering about, *"Stubborn women who never listen."* I got a great view of his well-developed, firm ass, and I liked to grab on to it as we moved. He, in turn, would slap my butt, resting his free hand on it to keep me in place.

At times, his caveman routine led to another "talk," and then he'd fuck me over the sofa, on the counter, or even against the door, before returning to the command center, leaving me blitzed and sated. I would have a short nap and sneak back downstairs.

It was just our thing.

But it didn't happen today. After I finished talking to Egan, I spoke to Damien and Leo, who were still digging for more information. I felt restless and edgy—it seemed strange to be in the command center without Marcus.

"Where do you think he is?" I asked Damien.

He smiled. "Sometimes when he gets too much in his head, he'll work out or spend time in his garden."

"I prefer it when he cooks," Leo said with a chuckle. "We all benefit then."

"Did something happen today that set him off?"

"Not that I know. I'm sure he is just clearing his head."

Leo grinned. "You wanna practice throwing your knife at my head?"

I laughed and shook my head. "No, I'm good."

He stood. "I'm going to head home, then. Dawn wasn't feeling overly well, and I want to check on her. Maybe pick up dinner so she doesn't have to."

Damien looked up with a smirk. "Home at four in the afternoon? And dinner? She'll be so shocked she might go into early labor."

Leo chuckled. "She would probably like that. She says she has no idea how she is going to make it another four weeks."

With a wave, he departed, and I left Damien and Egan still working. I climbed the steps, not surprised to find the apartment filled with appetizing aromas. Marcus was in the kitchen, a white apron tied around his waist, his shirt sleeves rolled up, and he was busy dicing something on the chopping board, the knife moving swiftly in a continuous pattern. Strangely, I could toss a knife with deadly accuracy, but chopping vegetables wasn't a forte of mine.

He glanced up with a smile. His hair was still damp, so I knew he'd worked out and showered before starting to cook. "I was wondering when you'd come find me," he teased. "You can never stay away too long."

I sniffed and slid onto one of the barstools he kept tucked under the counter. "You were hoping I'd leave you alone. Forget it, buddy, those days are over. You're stuck with me."

He leaned over the counter and kissed me hard. "Good." He slid a glass of wine my way, and I took it, sipping the dry, rich red with appreciation. Marcus had some great wines.

"What are you making?"

"Chicken piccata. Angel-hair pasta."

My stomach growled.

"I thought we'd eat upstairs."

"On the roof?"

He nodded, and I watched, fascinated, as the tips of his ears turned a dull red.

"I wanted to take you out, like a date, but I decided we should stick close to home. So, I brought the date to you," he said, not meeting my eyes.

"Marcus," I breathed out.

He lifted his gaze. "Soon, we can. Once this is done, I'll take you anywhere you want to go. But for tonight, I thought you'd like to eat outside, enjoy the air, see the stars, and maybe dance a little under the moonlight."

I was touched by his gesture. "I would love that." I glanced down. "Maybe I should change."

"Why don't you have a bath while I finish this? Take your wine and soak. I thought we'd eat about six, so you have lots of time."

I didn't offer to help him cook. That was his thing, and he did it far too well for me to try to interfere. He was organized and meticulous in the kitchen—much the same way he was in running his team.

"Okay."

He filled my glass and tapped it toward me. "Off you go."

I glanced over my shoulder before I left the room. He was busy, chopping, turning to stir the sauce, reaching for some fresh parsley he must have picked. Completely in control, happy in his element, and deep in concentration, he looked sexy with a towel thrown over his shoulder, his hair mussed, and an intense look on his face.

The sudden thought that he was mine, that he belonged to me, hit me, and I had to grab the doorframe in shock as those words permeated my mind. I had never belonged to anyone before. I had never loved anyone the way I loved Marcus. There was a deep, abiding sense of rightness when I looked at him. I saw a future with him. A different kitchen, with sunshine surrounding us, him cooking, me laughing and teasing him, little faces beaming up at us from their seats at the table. I shook my head—I had never thought about children of my own until now. But with Marcus, I could see them. Living our lives together. Building a home, a family. Growing old, sitting on the porch rocking, watching our grandchildren one day.

"Do you want children?" I asked.

He glanced up, startled to find me still there, as well as my out-of-the-blue question.

"Definitely."

"With me?"

He wiped his hands and crossed the room, standing in front of me. He cupped my cheeks between his large palms and bent to brush a kiss over my mouth. "I want everything with you, sweetheart. And soon, we'll sit down and figure it all out. Plan our future. But for tonight, I just want you beside me, eating the food I made you. Then I want to hold you in my arms for a while. Can we do that tonight?"

I wrapped my free hand around his wrist, meeting his intense, loving dark gaze.

"Yes."

He pressed another kiss to my mouth. "Good."

He'd thought of everything. A pretty table, a small bunch of flowers in the middle. A blanket to sit on afterward. The food was incredible, the wine he served cold and delicious. We talked about everything and nothing as we ate. He shared a few amusing stories of antics he'd gotten into as a kid.

"I drove my parents crazy, I think. I was always into something I shouldn't be. My mom was smart and decided to teach me how to cook. She knew it would occupy my mind and my hands, and I could get into less trouble."

"Did you love it right away?"

He pursed his lips, pausing to take a sip of wine. "Love is a strong word. It was better than having to do the dishes, which is what often happened. I wasn't so sure about it until I made my first marinara and my dad said it was better than his." He grinned. "Then, I was hooked. I was determined every dish be better. After that, it was hard to keep me out of the kitchen."

I twirled the angel-hair pasta, slowly chewing the delicious mouthful. "You learned well."

He watched me with an indulgent smile. "My parents would have loved you," he said quietly. "They would have been crazy with their affection."

"Were they?" I asked. "Affectionate, I mean?"

"Very. Hugs, kisses, praise. With each other. With my nonna. With me. My friends loved them." He studied me, his head tilted. "What about your grandmother?"

"She loved me," I said. "I knew that. But she wasn't much for hugs or kisses. I think she was too busy trying to keep life from beating us down. On occasion, she'd pat my cheek and say 'good girl,' but that was it, really. Kisses were rare. She'd tell me I was smart and clever. That I could do anything I set my mind to." I shrugged. "She tried."

"I think you turned out pretty well."

I smiled. "Sometimes I'd long for a hug or a snuggle. But I knew she didn't like it, so I never asked."

He met my eyes across the table. "You can ask me anytime."

The sincerity and simplicity of his words rang true. They brought a lump to my throat, and my eyes were damp as I smiled. "I'll remember that."

He crossed his arms, tapping his shoulders. "These are yours. Just say the word."

"Okay."

He cleared our plates and carried them downstairs. The sun was beginning to set as we ate dessert, the raspberry gelato sweet and tart on my tongue. Then he held out his hand and pulled me to my feet. We danced close in the waning light, and I sighed in contentment in his arms, my head resting on his chest, the sound of his steady heartbeat soothing under my ear.

"Great date," I whispered.

"Our first one," he replied.

"First of many."

He tightened his arms, and that was when I felt it. The tension in his body that had been growing during dinner. More than once, I had noticed his intense gaze directed my way, yet when I would meet his eyes, he would smile and blink, making me think I had imagined it.

What I didn't imagine was the hold he had on me. How close his embrace held me to his body. The stiffness of his shoulders I realized had been there all night. Something was wrong, and he wasn't telling me.

"Say it," I whispered. "Tell me what's wrong."

"Julian made contact with your captain."

I stopped moving, standing in the protective shelter of his arms, the world outside this moment suddenly invading our peace with a loud scream.

"When?"

"This afternoon."

"And?"

"He stated he was shocked but grateful to find out you were alive. He told Julian he would make the arrangements for your safe return to the States."

"So, we wait," I whispered.

"We wait," he said grimly.

I lifted my gaze to his, meeting his intense, steady gaze.

"I will protect you," he vowed.

"I know." I swallowed. "Take me downstairs, Marcus. Make love to me and hold me all night. Please."

"Missy, sweetheart—"

I cut him off with a shake of my head. "Please. I need to lose myself with you tonight. Reality will come soon enough."

He ran a finger down my cheek, nodding. Then he bent and swooped me into his arms and carried me downstairs to his bed, his mouth never leaving mine.

CHAPTER THIRTEEN

Marcus

The next morning, I met with Julian, and he informed me he'd received a call from Dan Jared.

"He told me Missy would be 'collected' on Friday."

"Two days from now," I said with a frown.

He nodded, looking grim. "We need to be ready."

"We are. The building is covered. You'll be there?"

We had decided my warehouse was the best place for this to happen. We knew every inch of the place and could cover it with the most efficiency.

He nodded. "I'll have extra men stationed like we planned. They'll be followed, but by so many cars they won't pick it up. Between that and the tracking chips, Missy won't slip through our fingers. Once they take her to Zander, we'll get him."

My gut churned at the thought of letting her out of my sight, but I nodded.

"How is she?" he asked.

"Terrified," I replied. "Trusting me to make sure she comes through this okay."

"She will." He studied me. "If you don't believe it, then we have a problem."

I tapped my chest, meeting his eyes. "The thought of him getting close to her does something to me in here. Simply the notion he could touch her, hurt her in any fashion, ties me in knots."

"Then stop thinking of her as Missy. Think of her as one of the other women you have helped. Step back personally. Otherwise, you're no good to her."

He was right, and I knew it. But I wasn't sure I could do that anymore. Missy had become part of me. I felt her pain and anxiety as if it were my own. Her joy made me happy; her laughter brought mine to the surface. Her worries and fears made me tense. Her certainty in me, in the fact that I would protect her and keep her safe, was both touching and terrifying. I wasn't sure what I would do if anything happened and she was taken from me. The urge to grab her and run was stronger than ever. It took all of my strength to tamp it down and follow through with the plan.

"I'm trying, Julian."

We shared a silent look of determination.

"Let's do this."

***

That afternoon, I worked at my desk, Missy in the chair in the corner. She was unusually quiet and pale. Her hair was down, the honey-red color catching the afternoon light. She had an open book on her lap but wasn't looking at it at all, instead staring out the window. Damien worked at his computer, Allen on the other side of the office. Leo had been called away by his wife, the call having come in moments after I came back from seeing Julian. He had picked up his phone, staring for a moment at his screen, then calling his wife and talking quietly. He hung up with a curse and stood, his face ashen and drawn.

"What is it?" I asked.

"I have to go," he said through tight lips. "Dawn isn't well."

I indicated the elevator. "Go. Keep me informed."

He nodded and hurried away. I hadn't heard from him yet, but I hoped she was okay. This was their first child, and he was naturally nervous.

Missy shifted, bringing my attention back to her. She was unnaturally still, her gaze focused on the outside.

"Hey," I called. "You want to do something?"

"Do something?"

"We could go for a drive," I suggested. As long as I was with her, she would be safe. "Get some ice cream?" Missy loved ice cream of any kind.

"You don't have time."

I stood. "For you, I do." It would do us both good to get out. See something other than the same four walls. We wouldn't be gone long, and it would help distract her. Break her out of the dark thoughts swirling in her head. The same ones that haunted mine.

I held out my hand. "Let's go."

We drove for an hour, finding a random ice cream place and eating cones in the sunshine of the late fall afternoon. The air was cool, but neither of us minded. The farther away we went from the warehouse, the brighter her smile got. The easier it became for me to breathe.

"When this is over, we're leaving," I announced.

"Leaving?" she asked, pausing between licks of her cone.

"Leaving. I'm taking you away."

"Away, where?"

I thought of the island Matteo and Evie lived on. The endless sunshine and peace they surrounded themselves with. It had never been something I craved before now, but at the moment, it was all I wanted. To see Missy in the sun, no worries or fears—the thoughts of a madman, darkness, and cages fading away to an obscure place in her mind.

"Somewhere warm, safe, and private."

"What about Hidden Justice?"

"I've done my time. It needs a new leader. A fresh set of eyes."

"I can't ask you to stop what you're passionate about for me."

I leaned over and kissed her, tasting the dark chocolate of her ice cream on her mouth. "I'm passionate about you. I want to build a life with you." I paused, uncertain suddenly. "As long as that is what you want."

She cupped my cheek, her small fingers soft on my skin. "It is. I don't want to be alone or invisible anymore."

"You'll never be invisible to me."

"I have some things of my gran's—"

I cut her off. "We'll figure it out. We'll get everything you want."

"It's only a couple of items. Sentimental ones."

"Whatever you want."

She smiled and offered me her mouth. I pressed mine to hers happily.

"Then take me wherever you want to, Marcus. We'll build a new life together."

"Done."

"I'll hold you to that."

I winked. "You do that, sweetheart."

She insisted on taking ice cream back, and when we arrived at the warehouse, she hurried ahead of me upstairs, and I stopped to drop off the treat she'd brought for Egan, figuring by now he'd be back in the basement. I entered his space, surprised not to see him bent over his laptop, then decided he must still be upstairs. By habit, my glance fell to the security monitors, and I frowned at the sight of the command center. It appeared empty.

Where the hell was everyone?

I watched in horror as Missy stepped from the elevator, looking around, the smile fading from her face. She rushed forward, dropping the bag she was carrying and covering her mouth at whatever she saw in front of her. She fell to her knees, out of sight, and I clicked the cameras, needing to see what had terrified her so much. She was leaning over the prone figure of a man, talking rapidly, running her hands over him. I recognized the jacket he wore, and with growing apprehension, I realized it was Leo. Beaten and bloodied on the floor of the command center. My fingers flew over the keyboard, examining every angle I could. Allen was on the floor, blood surrounding him. Egan wasn't far away, still and unmoving against a wall. Damien was slumped over his desk, his gun on the floor. Another man I didn't know was on the floor, more blood around his body.

But it was the still figure standing in my office doorway of the command center that grabbed my attention.

Tall, thin, with a headful of blond hair, the man I knew without a doubt was Xavier Zander was in the same room as Missy, having gotten into my building, killed my men, and had been waiting. For her.

I opened the hidden compartment behind me, choosing my weapons, even as I kept my attention on the screen in front of me. All my worry and stress evaporated, my focus narrowing to one single item. I felt a strange sense of calm as I chose my gun. I had one mission and that was to end that motherfucker.

He thought he was going to take her?

He was going to have to go through me first.

And he was going to lose.

MISSY

The sounds of footfalls make me look up from the nightmare that surrounded me. A tall, reedy man approached me, the look on his face making my blood run cold. I had only seen a grainy image of him, but I knew who he was.

Zander.

And he was here to get me.

I stood, the bag of ice cream lying at my feet, the top having broken open, the sweet custard melting on the floor.

He stopped a few feet away, his height imposing. His face was expressionless, the sharp angles and thin lips giving him an emaciated look. His eyes were green—flat and stony. Empty and terrifying. Bottled rage rolled off him, his long, skeletal fingers stroking the barrel of the gun he held. Blood was spattered on his jacket, and I wondered which of the men he had killed around me had dared to splash him. Which one of Marcus's men had killed the stranger on the floor before dying themselves.

"I've been waiting," he said. I had only heard his voice once, but any doubts of who he was fled as he spoke, the icy, removed tone making me shiver in memory. "I don't like to wait."

"Too fucking bad," I spat.

A smile split his mouth, looking odd on his thin face. It was cold and unfeeling. "Such language. I shall soon cure you of that."

I stepped to the right. "You won't have the chance to cure me of anything, asshole."

He laughed, the sound frightening. It was a sound of lunacy, high-pitched and eerie. He matched my movements, drawing closer with his longer legs. I shifted again, needing to put as much distance between us as possible. I had to give Marcus a chance to get to me.

Unless—

I put a stop to that train of thought. Marcus would be here in a moment.

We circled each other, me trying to figure out an escape route, him staring with those soulless eyes.

"Ah, Xyla," he murmured. "I have been in purgatory without you."

"I'm not your dead sister, you sick fuck," I hissed. "You're crazy."

For a moment, he said nothing, simply stared at me, his soulless eyes unnerving. I refused to let him see my anxiety, glaring back at him with all the hatred inside me for him plain to see.

"I am well aware you are not her," he replied calmly. "My sister, although perfect on so many levels, lacked one thing."

"A decent brother?" I snapped, hoping to make him angry. Force him to make a mistake.

He shook his head. "Mental strength. She was never able to see the big picture, to understand what we could have together. She fought what should have come so naturally to her." His smile twisted my stomach, making it queasy. "But she sent me you. You are her gift to me to make up for that weakness."

I gaped at him. He was even more deranged than I thought.

"I shall enjoy breaking you. Then once you accept your role, we'll move on to the next step."

"Which is me killing you?"

He lifted his arm, rubbing his chin with the barrel of his gun. I tried not to show my fear as he moved yet again, and I stepped back toward the long counter at the back wall. I needed to get there.

"Which is my seed in your womb. My son growing inside you. Xyla knew I needed someone stronger than she to carry on my legacy. She gave of her life so I could have it."

"She killed herself to get away from you, asshole."

For the first time, I saw him react. A visible shudder of anger raced through him, and his grip tightened on his gun. He lifted it, pointing it at my head.

"It was an accident. A tragic accident."

"Like your parents?" I said, sarcasm dripping from my mouth.

"They had to die. They were keeping us apart."

"She died to get away from you. She would rather have ended her life than give you want you wanted. She didn't want *you*," I sneered.

"You will shut your mouth."

"Or you'll kill me? I would far rather that than ever let you touch me. Just like Xyla," I mocked, knowing I was starting to anger him.

"I am going to do more than touch you. I am going to break you," he repeated. "You will feel my love as I beat it into your skin. The darkness of the cage you fear so much will become your friend, *Melissa*," he promised, his alarming words and low voice sending fear tearing through my body. I hated how my name sounded coming from his mouth. "There will be no one to save you this time. Your mind will bend, and you will bow to me. My wishes. You will forget anything else in this life but me. That is how I will honor Xyla. How I will fulfill the legacy I shared with her."

"I don't fucking think so," Marcus growled behind Zander. "The only thing that will be forgotten is your miserable life."

I had no idea where Marcus had come from. The elevator didn't open, the door to the stairway was shut, but he was here. He was alive.

Relief made tears spring to my eyes. It also distracted me, and I gasped as Zander spun and yanked me in front of him, using me as a shield, wrapping his hand around my neck to keep me in place.

"Get your disgusting hands off her."

Zander dragged me closer, the scent of him washing over me. I swallowed in revulsion as the overpowering stench of heavy spice and bitter lemon hit me. If evil had a smell, it was that. Cloying, unpleasant, and iniquitous. I twisted, trying to get away, and he tightened his grip, making me whimper in pain as his fingernails dug into my skin. He pressed his gun to my head, the cold metal burrowing into my skin.

"I wondered when you would arrive. I was hoping soon so I could let her watch you die."

"I'm here now. And I'm going to end *you*. You will never touch her again. Ever."

Zander shook his head. "Such brave words. I had heard so many rumors of the Hidden Justice." He smiled coldly. "How overstated they were. A few men, easily overtaken by brains and a plan. A simple plan *you* would never think of." He tapped his forehead. "Simple and brilliant. Arrive early. Take the girl. Kill you all. You didn't expect me, so you weren't ready." He shook his head, false pity saturating his words. "What a shame."

"Oh, I have a plan," Marcus assured him, his gaze never wavering. "And it's even simpler. Kill you."

Zander's evil laugh made me want to throw up. The ice cream I had eaten earlier turned sour in my stomach, making it ache. There was a malevolent air around him. It saturated everything. His face, his voice, his very presence. It radiated and made me physically ill. The mere thought of him even closer to me was abhorrent.

"How did you get in here anyway?" Marcus asked, looking calm.

"Everyone has a weakness. I found his." He indicated Leo. "I made his wife call him. I made sure he came to me. Then once he knew I had no problem killing her if he refused, he agreed to help me."

"And his reward was this?" Marcus crouched, touching Leo's neck. "He's barely breathing."

"That was his punishment for saying no the first time."

"And the rest of my men?"

"Because they were in my way. I'm not certain they're all quite dead yet. You interrupted my fun."

Marcus stood, his hatred evident in his glare. "You sick fuck. I'm going to enjoy killing you."

"And you call me delusional."

I tried to twist out of his grip, to give Marcus the chance to shoot him, but Zander's hold on my neck tightened to the point I could barely breathe. His fingers dug into my skin, his grip hard and painful, exactly the way I knew his touch would be. I felt his nails break the skin, the warm feel of my blood welling under his hold. I struggled against it, hating the feeling. I gasped for air, making Marcus angrier.

"*Get* your hands off her."

"She needs to get used to it. The collar I will keep her in until she breaks will be much tighter."

Fear and bravery combined inside me. I knew I had to fight—to risk everything if I wanted to live. I lifted my foot, stomping on Zander's instep. It jolted him enough he released me, although when I tried to run, he pushed me, sending me to the floor. I cried out as my head glanced off the hard surface of the counter, and I sank to the floor, the room spinning. I fought against it. I wasn't letting him win.

I had too much to lose.

CHAPTER FOURTEEN

Marcus

I was distracted seeing Missy fall, and my aim was off. Zander's bullets found purchase—one in my shoulder, the other in my chest. I gritted my teeth at the pain radiating in my torso. The force of the shots sent me down, and Zander rushed across the room, pushing me onto my back, his face ugly and twisted.

Zander straddled me, bending low to push his fist over top of the bloody hole on my shoulder and pressing down hard. The pain was red-hot and agonizing, and I couldn't help the groan that escaped.

"How the mighty have fallen. The hero of the hour about to die," he tsked. He bent lower as if telling me a secret, pressing his gun to my head. "Tell me, do you want to fuck every woman you save?"

"Only her," I snarled. "And I did. Many times. It was my name she moaned. The only one she ever will moan."

His furious gaze met my hate-filled one. He pressed the

gun harder. I knew he was itching to pull the trigger, but he wanted to torment me more first. I needed to keep him talking. To figure out a plan. To give Julian time to get here with backup.

"She's mine," I informed him. "She always will be."

"She will forget you ever existed," he mocked. "I'll make sure of that. I will brand her so deeply, your name will be erased."

"It's going to be the other way around," I replied, struggling against the pain and the blood soaking my shirt. "She hates you as much as your sister did."

His eyes flickered, loathing and anger spilling from them, and I knew I'd hit my mark. He pulled back, lifting his arm, no doubt planning on inflicting some more pain before he killed me. The familiar sound of a knife slicing through the air surprised me, but not as much as it did him. He arched his back as the blade sank deep into his shoulder, and a small grunt of pain escaped his mouth. Another grunt, louder this time, happened when the second blade found its home in the other shoulder. He looked shocked, confused, searching for the source of pain and the reason he was now incapable of lifting his arms.

A third knife sailed through the air, and I watched it, mesmerized by the beauty of its flight. An inhuman sound left his mouth, and his eyes bulged, confusion and pain making his expression almost comical. The silver tip of the knife sticking out the front of his throat glistened with his blood.

My beautiful, strong woman had incredible aim.

I pushed him with my working arm, and he fell backward, the force of his fall thrusting the blades deeper inside him. Robbing him of speech, breath, and blood. His mouth opened, nothing coming out but incoherent gurgles. I picked up my gun and staggered to my feet, staring into the fading gaze of the man who caused so much harm to others. Who would no longer be a threat to Missy or anyone. I felt nothing but relief. No regret for the pain he was in or the fact that he would be dead soon. He lifted his hands, clawing at the air, desperate to breathe. To escape the pain. A trickle of blood fell from his mouth.

"How the mighty have fallen," I mocked. "This was a simple plan too. I knew you would show up, and I knew you would try to take her." I smiled coldly, pulling aside my shirt so he saw the protective vest I wore. I'd known he wouldn't trust anyone else but himself to get her.

"I wasn't going to allow that to happen." I glanced over to the side of the room when movement caught my eye.

Damien lifted his head, confused but alive. The bulletproof vests I had insisted on protected my men. The same as mine had done for me. The fake blood pouches gave Zander a false sense of security, and our arrival had stopped him from finishing the job.

"You okay?" I asked, relieved.

Damien rubbed his head. "His guy pistol-whipped me. Egan shot him but took a couple of hits. Allen went down hard." He reached for his phone, wincing. "I'll call for a bus and backup."

My sternum hurt from the bullets, so I could sympathize. My shoulder was on fire, but I had to ignore it until this was done. I was relieved to know my men were injured but not dead.

The same would not hold true for Zander.

I switched my attention back to the man dying on the floor. I held the muzzle against Zander's head. "The devil is waiting, and he has a special place in hell for you," I promised. "I hope you enjoy burning for eternity." I smiled. "I'll be living a life with Missy, filling her days with love and sunshine. She'll never even think of you again. No one will even remember your name."

His pain-soaked wheezes filled the air, and he struggled to talk. I refused to give him the chance. I bent close.

"Sayonara, motherfucker. I got the girl. You die." I smirked. "I won." With a final glare, I pulled the trigger, silencing him forever.

His body jerked and spasmed, then melted onto the floor. The hole in his forehead was neat and tidy. Blood seeped from his other injuries. His breath gurgled and stopped. I had finished him.

That had been my one absolute order. Unless it put Missy's life in danger, I had to be the one to kill him.

And I had done it.

I collapsed, the world spinning out of control. I heard voices and running feet. Suddenly, Julian was there, barking orders, Missy hovering over me, begging me to stay, not to leave her.

I tried to tell her I wasn't going anywhere. That I was fine. I'd been shot before and survived. But my tongue felt strangely thick, and I couldn't seem to form the words.

Then my world became quiet and dark.

The last thing I heard was Missy crying.

I opened my eyes to an unfamiliar room. The light was dim, and a thick, medicinal smell surrounded me. I focused on the pale-green walls with recognition. I was in a hospital room—which meant I was alive.

I took stock of my body, feeling the lingering soreness in my chest and the more pronounced pain in my shoulder. My arm was in a sling, and thick bandages were encasing my shoulder. An IV was hooked into my other arm, and if I was being honest, I ached all over. I was getting too old to keep getting shot.

I turned my head, my anxiety easing as soon as I saw her. Missy was in the chair beside my bed, asleep. I studied her anxiously, my anger flaring as I saw the marks that scum had left on her. Fresh bruises were on her arms and head, and her neck was mottled with dark contusions and small cuts. I made a noise in my throat that sounded suspiciously like a growl. Part of me wanted to find out Zander was alive so I could kill him all over again—this time taking my time.

Missy sat upright, her gaze finding mine in the dim light. Her lovely eyes were red-rimmed and damp, letting me know how much she'd been crying.

"Hey, sweetheart," I rasped out. "It's okay."

She stood, hovering over me. "That's what I am supposed to say to you."

"Sorry." I cleared my throat. "Is there water around?"

She poured a cup and held the straw as I sipped the cool liquid gratefully. I lifted my hand, stroking her cheek. "Any chance of a mint?"

She frowned. "A mint? I don't think I can give you that until the doctor clears you."

"Too bad," I grumbled. "I really want to kiss you, but I'm sure my breath—"

She cut me off, pressing her mouth to mine. Our lips moved and caressed, neither of us trying to deepen it, just needing the feel of the moment between us.

She lifted her head, and I smiled. "Thanks. I needed that."

"Me too."

I cupped her face again. "No more crying."

"No more getting shot," she replied.

"Deal." I groaned as I moved. "Jesus, it feels like I got hit by a truck."

"That happens when you tangle with bad men."

I met her eyes. "Not anymore," I said, making her a silent promise.

She nodded, holding my hand to her face.

"Leo?" I asked. "The others?"

"Everyone is okay," she replied. At my dubious look, she smiled. "I promise. A little worse for wear, but okay."

Julian walked in, looking relieved when he saw me awake. "Well, there he is."

"Hey," I greeted him, my voice still hoarse.

Missy stepped back, my hand dropping from her face. "I'll go get the doctor."

"Okay."

Julian put his hand on her shoulder. "Why don't you go and get something to eat. The boys are already downstairs."

He looked at me. "She hasn't left your side."

She glanced my way, and I nodded. "Go."

She picked up her purse and left, her glance lingering. I smiled to reassure her, but as soon as the door shut, I turned my attention to Julian.

"Leo?"

"He was beaten badly, but he'll be okay." He paused. "Eventually."

"His wife? The baby?" I knew if anything happened to them, Leo would never recover.

"We found her tied up and frightened, but unharmed. I think that scum had other plans for later, but he never lived to see them. She's in labor now. Leo is with her."

"Will she be okay? The baby?"

"The doctor was sure both would be fine. Leo will heal, but I doubt he'll return."

I wasn't surprised to hear that news. Julian would find him a good job elsewhere where he would be safe.

"Zander—he is dead, then?"

Julian smirked. "Between the knives in his back and neck and the bullet between his eyes? I doubt even the devil himself could resurrect him."

"And my men?"

"All shot. All saved by the vests. Egan took two hits—one high on his shoulder, which threw him into the wall, knocking him out cold. Allen was shot, but the vest took it. He hit the desk on the way down. There was enough blood to convince the asshole to turn his attention to Damien. But, again, you interrupted his plans." He met my eyes. "But they all survived, Marcus. Your insistence on the vests saved them. The new technology of the vests helped. I'm not sure the older ones would have worked with the bullets Zander liked to use at such close range."

"Is that why I fucking hurt so much?"

"Yes. They had to do a lot of digging to get it out as well."

"Great," I grunted.

I shifted, trying to get comfortable. "The leak? Her captain?" I asked.

"Caught trying to get away. Arrested and facing a multitude of charges. I doubt he'll see the outside of a prison again." Julian shrugged. "Or live long enough to worry about it. Inmates don't tolerate cops inside very well. Lots of accidents happen even if they're kept separated."

I had zero sympathy for the scumbag, but before I could say anything else, the door opened.

The doctor walked in, frowning at Julian. "Really? He just woke up. Your questions can't wait?"

"I'm here as a friend," Julian lied smoothly.

The doctor examined me and asked a lot of questions. Finally, he was done, tucking the tablet under his arm. "You're a lucky man, Mr. Gallo. A fraction of an inch over, you would have bled out before you got here. As it was, it nicked an artery—you're lucky to be alive. You lost a lot of blood and you're going to be sore, but you'll heal."

"When can I get out of here?"

"When I say so. You just woke up. We need to make sure everything is okay, set you up with physio, and then you'll be discharged."

"Today," I insisted.

"Not happening. Perhaps in the next forty-eight hours." The doctor turned and walked out the door.

"Do something about that," I grumbled. "Get me out."

"No way. Missy would kill me with one of her fancy knife moves."

"Coward."

"Yep." He grinned.

For a moment, there was silence before he spoke.

"How did you know he'd show up? To insist on vests?"

I sighed. "I didn't, but I had a feeling he might. As Missy pointed out, he was obsessed. And she'd slipped through his fingers once—he wasn't taking the chance again. By taking her himself, he was certain he'd have her. When you said Friday, I wondered why so long, then I decided to be prepared. He thought he'd catch us unawares, and in some ways, he did. I never thought of protecting the men outside the building. I had no idea he'd use a pregnant woman to get to us. I should have, I suppose."

"You can't think of everything, Marcus."

I drank some water to relieve my dry throat. "Have the men told you what happened?" I asked.

"Basically what you saw and already figured out, I think. Zander lured Leo out with his wife, then threatened to kill her unless he took them into the building. Once they were inside and Leo was no longer needed, they beat him, tossed him out of the elevator to startle everyone, and opened fire. Your men shot back and killed Zander's guy before they were all injured. He waited." He brushed a hand over his head. "It's lucky you weren't there."

"I took Missy for ice cream to get her mind off things."

"Good thing."

"I suppose in the end, yes."

For a moment, I closed my eyes, exhaustion bearing down on me. The next thing I knew, Missy was beside me, stroking my head.

"Where's Julian?"

"He left over an hour ago. He'll be back."

"I won't be here."

She crossed her arms. "Yes, you will be. Your ass isn't leaving this hospital until the doctor signs off and I'm okay with it."

"I don't recall you ranking over me, Missy."

She leaned down. "I outrank you in every way right now, buddy. I'm on my feet, no bandages, no IV, and I can pee on my own. Once you get three of the four, you can go home. Not a second sooner. Hear me?"

Her bossiness made me smile, but I hid it. It was adorable, sweet, comforting, and a bit of a turn-on if I was being honest. I lifted my hand and stroked her cheek.

"Will you stay with me?"

She wrapped both hands around mine and squeezed. "Yes."

I sighed. "Okay, then. You win."

She sniffed. "That's the way it's gonna be from now on. Get used to it."

Once again, I hid my smile.

I was good with that.

CHAPTER FIFTEEN

Marcus

Sunlight played on the sand, picking out spots to shine on like diamonds on the fine granules. I lifted my face to the warmth of the sun, enjoying the heat. Peace surrounded me, the only sounds the gentle waves kissing the shore and the muted laughter of children playing in the distance. Entwined with it was Missy's amusement, and the happy sounds made my lips turn up into a smile. I could never resist her laughter.

"There you are," Matteo said, sitting down beside me on the beach. "I wondered if you'd disappeared over here again."

"Over here" was a small stretch of beach around a bend on the island Matteo, Evie, and their family lived on. Three other couples lived there too, all of whom I knew and had worked with when I was with Matteo's team. Geo and Lila, Vince and Gianna, and Alex and Roza had all joined Matteo here to live out their lives in harmony and warmth. Thousands of miles from the blood and violence their world had contained. They rebuilt their worlds one happy memory at a time.

"It's a great spot."

He nodded, not saying anything for a moment. When he spoke, his voice was serious. "It's yours, Marcus. For you and Missy if you want it. We'll build a house. You can move here and let the sun and tranquility heal you." He paused. "If you're ready."

"Missy is. I want to give her back her peace of mind." I rubbed the back of my neck. "She loves it here."

We'd arrived a month ago. I was still recovering, and she was terrified unless I was by her side. Her nightmares had returned full force, and I had been at a loss as to how to help her. I'd thought knowing she'd had a hand in Zander's demise would bring her closure, but it only seemed to make things worse. Two weeks after we arrived, I found her sobbing on the beach late at night, and she'd finally confessed her nightmares hadn't been about Zander, but about me.

"In my dreams, I miss and you die," she sobbed. "I lost you."

I wrapped her in my arms. "No, sweetheart. I'm right here. Feel me." I laid her hand over my heart. "Feel that. I'm strong. I'm good."

"I miss you," she sniffled, her voice quiet. "I keep thinking, somehow, something I've done has made you change the way you feel about me."

"Never," I vowed, stroking along her chin.

"You haven't touched me."

My fingers stilled. "I wanted to give you time," I confessed. "Between my shoulder and the trauma you experienced, I thought maybe you didn't want that yet. Or ever again," I admitted.

Her beautiful eyes shone with unshed tears. "I want you more than ever."

I covered her mouth with mine, and I kissed her. I didn't stop until we were naked, the gentle breeze blowing around our overheated skin. I carried her to the ocean and made love to her, letting the warm water wash away her fears and my touch bring her back to reality. Back to me. That was the last nightmare she'd experienced. We'd both turned a page and began to heal.

"What about you?" Matteo asked. "Are you ready?"

"I think so. I'm tired of the dark. You used to say that, and I never fully understood. I do now. I want to live without fear. Without blood. Without every thought in my mind something shadowy and twisted."

"But?" he prompted.

"I'm worried, Matteo. What if I'm no good at it? What if I can't settle the way you have? What if I'm a terrible partner for Missy?" I barked out a laugh. "I never expected to fall in love. Never planned on giving up my path so early in life. I thought I'd outlast everyone. I had nothing else."

"Until her," he finished.

"Until her," I agreed.

"Hurts to admit you're not as tough as you thought you were, doesn't it?" He chuckled then became serious. "I never planned on Evie, but she is the best thing that ever happened to me. She and our children fill me with a satisfaction I never found on the job." He leaned forward, meeting my eyes. "It is never going to end, Marcus. The chase. The need to move on to the next case, the next bad guy, the next victim. All you can do is give what you can until you can't give anymore. Frankly, I think you already know the answer. I think you want this, you're just afraid to ask for it."

"Maybe."

"It's true. I'm right on this subject."

I glanced at him. "You think you're pretty smart, don't you?"

His lips quirked. "Evie says I am. And show some respect. I'm still the boss, and you're my second."

The sounds of feminine voices approaching made me smile. "I think the real boss and second are coming this way."

He chuckled. "I think so too." He clapped me on the shoulder. "Make this your home, Marcus. Talk to Missy. Leave her here so you know she is safe, and return to Canada and get your affairs in order. Leave that life behind. Come back unhindered and find a new path." He extended his arm, sweeping it as if showing off the view. "Grab happiness and celebrate the second chance you were given."

My gaze fell on Missy as she walked toward us. She was wearing a pretty sundress that left her shoulders and neck bare. Her skin was sun-kissed, and she looked healthy. Happy. She got along well with the women, was well-liked by the men, and adored by the children. And she returned their affection completely.

Matteo was right.

It was time.

MISSY

"Live here? Permanently?" I asked, unsure I had heard correctly.

Marcus tilted his head, confused. "I thought you liked it here."

"I do, but Marcus, is that what you want?"

He paced around on the beach, his hands clasped behind his back. He had healed well, but I still saw the occasional grimace of pain cross his face. Watched as memories weighed heavy on his mind. He stopped his pacing to stand in front of me. He lowered himself to the blanket I was sitting on.

"What I want is to live with you without fear. Without wondering what horrors I will uncover tomorrow that might take me away. I never want to see you worry and suffer because I walk out the door and you're terrified I won't come back," he said with conviction.

He swept out his arm. "This place. This place can help us heal, Missy. We could build a life here. Or, if you want, just stay for a couple of years, then move on. Matteo has offered me this stretch of beach. We can have a house built and settle down or settle for now. As long as you're with me, I don't care."

"What about the team? Julian?"

"I doubt Julian will be surprised. Leo won't return—I already know that. Damien wants to step back and go more behind the scenes. Egan can have any position he wants with the agency. They'll find their own path." I shrugged. "Or not. We all have to make our decisions based on what is best for ourselves—not the team. Eventually, the two have to separate." He blew out a long breath. "And Julian will decide what is best for Julian. Maybe one day he'll find his reason to walk away. At least, I hope he does. It's a lonely, isolated life otherwise."

"Like you did?"

He touched my cheek tenderly. "Yes. The bottom line is, I think eventually he'll find he's given all he has to give. Like I did. Like Matteo. But he has to do it in his own time."

He wrapped his hands around mine. "Say yes, Missy. Stay here with me. I love you. And you're more important than anything else. Stay. Marry me. Make babies with me. Boss me around. Put me in my place. Anything you want, as long as you stay with me."

"And we'll build a house here?"

"Yes. One filled with light. A place you can see the stars every night, watch the sunrise every day. A big kitchen for me—a place to garden. We'll plan it and build it together."

Tears glimmered in my eyes. "I can boss you around anytime?"

He laughed and kissed my mouth, his lips lingering. "Yes." He winked. "I don't promise to obey, but that's what makes us so great."

"I do like make-up sex."

"I like any kind of sex with you."

"How about celebration sex?" I asked.

He stilled, meeting my eyes. "Are we celebrating?"

"Yes," I said simply.

Immediately, I was under him on the blanket. "Then get ready to find out what celebration sex is like, sweetheart. I plan on celebrating hard."

His mouth descended on mine, claiming and possessive. Warm and teasing. Giving and loving. Smiling and happy. I could feel his love in his kiss. His promise of a new life in the shelter and safety of his arms.

That was all I needed.

EPILOGUE

Two Years Later

MISSY

I walked down the beach, my feet sinking into the warm sand. The breeze lifted my hair from my neck, the cool air feeling good on my skin. Absently, I rubbed my growing belly, smiling as I felt the push of a tiny hand or foot. I never knew. I was convinced this baby did backflips all the time. Even the doctor admitted he had never known one to be so active.

Our daughter was going to take after me.

I rounded the corner, pausing. Marcus sat on the deck of our house, his posture relaxed, a book on his lap. On the table beside him was a pitcher and two glasses, the red color of the contents bright in the sun. No doubt he had made another batch of his nonalcoholic sangria for me. Just blended fruit juice with tonic, really—but I loved it. So did the baby. She demanded it constantly. That and Marcus's Alfredo. I needed it every day. And every day without fail, he smiled, kissed me, and pulled out the pans.

Seeing our home always brought a smile to my face. Two stories, rustic, with lots of wood and stone, it matched the other houses on the island. Inside was simple and open. A living/dining area and huge kitchen took up most of the main floor. Marcus had an office he used only on occasion. Upstairs were four bedrooms and baths. Windows and slide-away doors that were more often open than not filled the main floor with sun and the sound of the waves and breeze. Simple furniture, light walls, and thick wood floors made it warm and inviting. We had a garden Marcus puttered in daily, providing everyone on the island with herbs and local vegetables. All the children loved to help him, and he enjoyed spending time with them.

The intense, on-guard man who had rescued me had changed. Gone was the perpetual frown, the constant worry, and the stress. He smiled more, laughed often, but still scowled and grumbled when I pissed him off.

Which I did often since I found his scowling, growling side very sexy. Luckily, it didn't take much. I knew what buttons to push. And it always ended up with make-up sex, which I had discovered was one of my favorites— although any time I had Marcus pressed against me naked was a favorite.

As if sensing me, he looked up, standing and setting his book on the table. He walked down the steps, heading my way. My breath caught in my throat as I watched him stroll toward me. Tall, proud, his skin a dark honey from the sun, his hair lighter from the time outdoors, and his muscles rippling as he moved, he was sex on legs and, even after two years, I found it hard to believe he was mine.

He reached me, bending to press a lingering kiss to my mouth, his hands cradling my rounded stomach.

"How are my girls?"

I grinned. "Thirsty. Hungry, too."

"What a shock." He chuckled as he wrapped an arm around my waist, tugging me toward the deck. "I have something to help with both of those."

He settled me into my favorite chair and handed me a tall glass of the juice. I sipped it, watching with delight as he left, returning quickly with two bowls. The Alfredo and penne were studded with chicken and broccoli, smelling incredible, the garlic and cheese wafting up from the steam.

"You knew I was coming?"

He laughed. "Evie radioed you were on your way. She said you'd mentioned you were hungry—twice."

"I ate there too. She gave me a grape jelly sandwich—well, two of them—and they were good, but our girl needs pasta."

He chewed and swallowed. "Every pregnancy, her cravings were the same. Grape jelly sandwiches and milk. Matteo could barely keep it in the house." He lifted an eyebrow. "Much the same way you keep me slaving away in the kitchen with your demand for fresh pasta and Alfredo."

I snorted around a mouthful. "You love it in your kitchen."

He leaned close and kissed me. "I do. I love you as well."

I smiled at him. "I know. I love you right back." I patted my stomach where the skin jumped. "We both do."

MARCUS

I glanced up from my book, unable to contain my smile. Missy was asleep in her chair, her head back on the pillow I had tucked behind her, her hands folded over our daughter, who appeared to be sleeping inside her momma, safe and, for the moment, sated with pasta and juice. It was rare not to see movement rippling under Missy's skin, a hand or foot pushing, getting ready to join us, although we still had six weeks left until her due date.

I was quite convinced she wouldn't wait that long. Even the doctor was prepared for this to be an early baby.

The breeze caught my wife's hair, stirring it around her peaceful face. The honey had lightened with all the time she spent in the sun, yet the red hue had deepened, and it was a stunning combination. I loved her hair. She had let it grow, and it now hung halfway down her back, a thick ribbon of ever-changing sunrise. She had filled out, and her face and eyes had lost that haggard, frightened look she had carried for so long.

After we'd made our decision to live here, Matteo took charge, and plans for the house were quickly drawn up. As difficult as it was, I left Missy here under his care and returned to Canada to close out my life there. Julian hadn't been happy, nor was he surprised by my resignation. He shook my hand and wished me well. None of my team stayed, scattering to the wind and other lives, except for Damien. He moved to Julian's office and became his right-hand, concentrating on computers and systems, tracking down leads. Julian trusted him implicitly.

I worked as quickly as I could, anxious to return to Missy. The warehouse was emptied, and I gave it to Julian for whatever use he could find for it, my possessions mostly sold except for personal items, and I arranged for Missy's few boxes to be shipped to me and closed out her apartment in the States.

Then I boarded a plane and returned to the woman who changed my life. When I held her in my arms again, I knew I would never leave her side again voluntarily. We married in a quiet ceremony and began anew, leaving the past where it belonged—in the past.

On this island, filled with endless sunshine and warmth, the small group of people became our family. We bonded more than ever, gathered strength from each other. Missy blossomed, discovering friendship and common ground with the women. Matteo and I worked with Gianna, once again putting our talent for making money to work on the fund. The work kept me involved but out of danger. It took a little while to break through Gianna's walls, but we were now close, and I would protect her as fiercely as Missy. Gianna was like a sister to me—much like Evie, whom I bonded with all over again once we settled. She and Missy were close, which made me happy.

Life was good.

I shook my head with a chuckle as I looked around.

No, life was great.

I saw Missy's dress ripple over her stomach, like a small wave cresting under her skin. My daughter was waking up.

Once again, I smiled.

Soon, it would be perfect.

———

Thank you so much for reading SECOND-IN-COMMAND. If you are so inclined, reviews are always welcome by me at your eretailer.

Next in the series is the leader who has watched his men fall in love, one by one - THE COMMANDER.

If you would like to read more in romantic suspense, BENTLEY is an opposites attract with a heroine who is an even match for our hero.

Enjoy reading! Melanie

COMING SOON

The Commander

The Present
Julian

I reached for a file, trying not to curse under my breath. Then I recalled I had a private office so I could curse all I wanted.

"Fucking paperwork," I snarled. "It never ends."

I picked up my coffee, cursing yet again when I realized the cup was empty. I punched the intercom, waiting until my secretary responded.

"Yes, sir?"

I managed to keep my voice civil. "Coffee, Anne. Now."

"Right away. A sandwich, perhaps?"

"Is it lunchtime?"

"It's two o'clock."

I shook my head in disbelief. The days passed in a rush of moments, it seemed.

It was a shame the nights dragged so badly.

"I would appreciate that."

I hung up before she could respond. She was an older woman, happy to have a job, not caring about the dull work she processed daily. She had no idea what really happened in the office behind her, and it was best kept that way. I had learned my lesson once.

Anne came in at ten, left at four, and when she wasn't typing or filing, getting me lunch or coffee, she kept herself busy by knitting. I didn't care. She was a cover, and it worked well for both of us.

An hour later, I finished signing all the papers, and I shoved them out of the way, running a hand over my eyes. I looked over at the sandwich sitting on the edge of my desk, the edges curling and drying, and I tapped the plate, knocking it into the garbage can.

My phone rang, and I answered it tersely.

"Julian Grayson."

"Yeah, boss, it's Conrad Baines."

Conrad was one of my security men. An excellent ex-agent and happily working in another capacity for me—but he was on leave. "Conrad, what's up?"

"I'm here at the London airport, waiting to leave."

I blinked, unsure what that had to do with me. "Okay."

"We like to fly out of here. Smaller than Toronto, you know? No crowds, no lineups."

"Yes, I understand," I said impatiently. I didn't really have time for idle chitchat about airports in Canada. But his next words hit me like a freight train.

"I saw her, Boss."

"Saw who?"

"Your wife."

My body locked down.

My wife. I hadn't heard those words in months.

"My ex, you mean," I said numbly, feeling the shock of his words. We weren't even technically divorced, but I let people think that way. It was easier.

I hadn't been able to find her since the day she'd walked out. It was as if she had disappeared. And for him to have spotted her?

What were the chances?

I realized he was still talking.

"The reason I noticed her, Boss, aside from the red hair, that is, was the fact that she had someone with her."

My stomach tightened.

She was with someone? Was that why she really left me?

"Oh?" I managed to get out.

"Yeah. She was carrying a baby, Boss. Like, a four-month-old baby. And the baby—she looked just like you. I'd recognize those eyes anywhere."

His words exploded in my head. They echoed and ricocheted around my brain, growing and expanding every second.

Wife.

Baby.

Four months.

She.

Eyes.

Looked like you.

I was on my feet in a second, standing so fast my chair hit the wall.

"Do you know what flight she's waiting for?"

"Same as ours. She'd headed to the Maritimes." He rattled off a number.

"Keep her in your sight," I snarled. "Don't let her see you."

"Good thing the plane is late—"

"It's going to be a lot later. Sorry."

I slammed down the phone, not waiting for him to respond. I pressed another button, already speaking before the person answering finished his greeting.

"I need Flight WJ873, departing London, Ontario, grounded until I get there. Mechanical issue—whatever you need to say for it to stay on the ground. Keep the passengers calm and in the terminal."

I hung up again and made another call.

"I need a helicopter. Now."

ACKNOWLEDGMENTS

Thank you to my wonderful readers who came along for
this ride into Canadian gray.
I hope you enjoyed it!

Lisa—your notes during this series made me smile.
Thank you for your endless patience.
I,love,you,and,thank,you,for,your,comma,lessons.
Pretty,sure,I,nailed,it.

Beth, Trina, Melissa, Sharon, Barbara, Carol, and Deb
—thank you for your valuable input, your keen eyes, and
encouragement. Your humor and help are so
appreciated.

Karen—For someone who uses words so much, when it
comes to you there simply
Not enough of them. Thank you, my friend. Love you
to the moon and back.

Kim—You are such a joy. Thank you for being part of the team and all you do.

My reader group, Melanie's Minions—love you all.

Melanie's Literary Mob—my promo team—you do me proud and I love our interactions.
You are my happy place and I love sharing time with you.
Your support is amazing and humbling.

To all the bloggers, grammers, ticktok-y-ers. Thank you for everything you do. Shouting your love of books—of my work, posting, sharing—your recommendations keep my TBR list full, and the support you have shown me is deeply appreciated.

And my Matthew—my everything. Always. Thank you.

ALSO AVAILABLE FROM MORELAND BOOKS

Titles published under M. Moreland

Insta-Spark Collection

It Started with a Kiss

Christmas Sugar

An Instant Connection

An Unexpected Gift

Harvest of Love

Titles published under Melanie Moreland

The Contract Series

The Contract (Contract #1)

The Baby Clause (Contract #2)

The Amendment (Contract #3)

Vested Interest Series

BAM - The Beginning (Prequel)

Bentley (Vested Interest #1)

Aiden (Vested Interest #2)

Maddox (Vested Interest #3)

Beneath the Scars

Over the Fence

My Image of You (Republishing 2022)

Changing Roles

Happily Ever After Collection

Revved to the Maxx

Heart Strings

ABOUT THE AUTHOR

NYT/WSJ/USAT international bestselling author Melanie Moreland, lives a happy and content life in a quiet area of Ontario with her beloved husband of thirty-plus years and their rescue cat, Amber. Nothing means more to her than her friends and family, and she cherishes every moment spent with them.

While seriously addicted to coffee, and highly challenged with all things computer-related and technical, she relishes baking, cooking, and trying new recipes for people to sample. She loves to throw dinner parties, and enjoys traveling, here and abroad, but finds coming home is always the best part of any trip.

Melanie loves stories, especially paired with a good wine, and enjoys skydiving (free falling over a fleck of dust) extreme snowboarding (falling down stairs) and piloting her own helicopter (tripping over her own feet.) She's learned happily ever afters, even bumpy ones, are all in how you tell the story.

Melanie is represented by Flavia Viotti at Bookcase Literary Agency. For any questions regarding subsidiary or translation rights please contact her at flavia@bookcaseagency.com

Connect with Melanie

Like reader groups? Lots of fun and giveaways! Check it out Melanie Moreland's Minions

Join my newsletter for up-to-date news, sales, book announcements and excerpts (no spam). Click here to sign up Melanie Moreland's newsletter

or visit https://bit.ly/MMorelandNewsletter

Visit my website www.melaniemoreland.com

facebook.com/authormoreland

twitter.com/morelandmelanie

instagram.com/morelandmelanie

Made in the USA
Middletown, DE
21 November 2021

53029432R00139